SADDL
IN THE KITCHEN

by

ENGA SMITH

Best wishes - Enga Smith

HESPERIAN PRESS

1993
HESPERIAN PRESS
P.O. BOX 317
VICTORIA PARK 6100
65 OATS STREET
CARLISLE 6101
WESTERN AUSTRALIA.

First published by Artlook 1979

ISBN 0 85905 191 9

By the same author
Mostly Good Times (1986)

Cover drawing by David Bornshin

Hesperian books are available direct from the publisher, but see your local bookshop first. For a full catalogue of Hesperian books on Australiana, natural history, exploration, Aboriginal ethnography, bush verse and gold prospecting please forward a self-addressed stamped envelope to the above address.

"Oh, those sparkling, halcyon days when the sun shone after rain and we were charmed by the simplest pleasure. We envied no-one anything,' in fact, we were sorry for anyone who wasn't us!"

Margaret, Bob, Jenny and Enga.
Playing near the creek.

CHAPTER 1

There was often a saddle in the kitchen in my earliest memories of home. The one I remember best was the small, shiny one given to my eldest sister, Margaret, by an aunt for her tenth birthday and when not in use, it rested jauntily with its checked saddlecloth on a stout peg on the kitchen wall, brand new and smelling wonderfully of good leather. New things came our way but rarely then, so, not surprisingly, it was thought to be far too superior to go out on the side verandah with the rest of Dad's worn selection. Other oddments of harness and horse gear festooned those unlined, white-washed iron walls in the kitchen; a bridle, a couple of pairs of hobbles and one stockwhip at least, whilst on the high, old-fashioned white pine dresser, along with tobacco tins of nuts and screws and drying pumpkin and melon seeds, were tall bright yellow containers of medication - Flint's, I believe "for the relief of sand in horses".

There was also a slender, blue castor oil bottle on the dresser, from which Dad swigged whenever he felt the need, to Mother's remonstrances of, "Oh Stuart - that's no way to take medicine. You'll harm yourself man!" His only answer would be a wink, a smack of the lips and another defiant swig. Somewhere too amongst this motley collection was the noisy cowbell Mother used to summon us to meals when we were working or playing away from the house and a tall, brass shell case, a legacy from the Great War, served in its retirement as a holder for pens and pencils, gleaming from a lower shelf.

But before I go any further with my descriptions of home, I'd better backtrack to the beginning; the years following the war. Dad, who'd fought with the Artillery in the trenches of France, was granted through the Soldier Settlement Scheme, just over two thousand acres amongst the flat topped hills outside Geraldton. There was nothing on the place, no wells, fences or dwelling; one had to take an axe and a waterbag and go to it. The scrub was thick and the age-old hills as hard as Hades but eventually some land was cleared, post holes punched down and fences erected. Later the tops of these hills were to form a great proportion of our best grazing and cropping land but the slopes were always difficult to muster and manoeuvre heavy machinery up and down. Nature compensated us well though for these drawbacks with wonderful look-out spots over the sea and surrounding countryside - away to the blue distance as far as the eye could see and the pale mauve-flowered wild hibiscus that thrived in the gravelly outcrops.

Ancient "blackboys" stood starkly silhouetted on the skyline, timeless sentinels guarding the valley beyond the paddock where an old shearing shed had once stood and in spring, pink heather and yellow Morrison blossomed in the valley, filling the air with sweetness as we rode through it and our horses' shod hooves crunched into the damp, rock-strewn earth below. There were caves in some of the hills that were big enough to stand up in and smelt of moss and fox and others, shallower, looking out towards the sea, that had tiny shells embedded in the walls and sprinkled in fragments through the fine dust on their floors; a tangible reminder of the long-ago time when the whole area had been under the ocean.

In January, nineteen twenty-six, my parents were married and went to live in a small, damp, tree-ringed cottage a mile or two from our farm. Dad worked the place from there for a couple of years before they moved to the three mud-floored, unlined rooms that were to form the nucleus of the home we knew. The rest grew with the family. Life must have been far from easy for Mother, a town girl and no longer in her first youth, having spent that in helping her own mother raise younger brothers and sisters. However, she settled down to have and raise the five of us - Margaret within the year and Bob, Jenny and myself, and David after that.

In those early days, and in fact for a great deal of our childhood, there was no water laid on to the house at all so there were no taps or sink in the kitchen. Washing-up was done in a large enamel basin which stood on a cupboard made up of pieces of packing case and was mercifully hidden from close scrutiny by green patterned oil-cloth. Pots, pans and bread tins were stacked on a shelf in this unbeautiful creation and dishwater had to be emptied out some distance from the back door where a forest of weeds we called marshmallows flourished greedily. Once Mother's wedding ring slipped off her soapy finger as she emptied the dish and we all had to poke about for days amongst the marshmallows before the search was abandoned. We never found the ring and Mother had to wait a long time until Dad could afford a replacement.

On days when butter was no more than a saffron puddle in the clay butter cooler on the kitchen table and the door to the east was open, the hot, restless wind skirled the dry leaves from under the big gum trees outside, right into the kitchen. A large, wood-burning, black stove with ample hobs on either side stood in one corner, a killer in summer heat but a blessing when chilly winter winds hooted through nail holes in the walls and slid under ill-fitting doors, and most of all when rain rattled on the corrugated iron roof. On mornings like this, we children squabbled amongst ourselves as to whose turn it was to make the toast, crouching as close as we could to the warmth with our bare feet on the open oven door and holding the bread over the coals on long-handled forks made of fencing wire. Shelves lined with scalloped newspaper ran along one section of the wall down the stove end of the kitchen and there were two pine tables, the larger surrounded by a collection of ricketty chairs, most of them reinforced in at least one juncture by a twitch or two of wire.

Outside the kitchen door, the wide verandah that ran around two sides of the house, was originally floored with hard, red mud, but was later cemented.

Norwest creeper spread its dense, dark foliage and soft crimson fruit thickly across the front section of the verandah. "Rats! Full of rats!" Grandpa declared vehemently and often as he sat in his latter days, erect and stiff-backed in his old cane-bottomed chair. Only occasionally he'd deign to use the more comfortable broad-armed, low-lung squatter's chair that stood permanently on the verandah in the shade of the creeper. A water-bag, suspended from a rafter, swung damp and bloated in any passing breeze, the rain water in it cool and infinitely refreshing.

Swallows twittered and squabbled in their muddy, cup-shaped nests in the rafters outside the sleepout door and made a mess on the floor below. Every season when the youngsters had left the nests, Mother would knock them down and scrub the verandah for a brief respite before the determined little creatures, not to be discouraged, winged in triumphantly bearing their assorted building materials, and so the cycle began again. The sleepout itself was a long, dormitory type of room, cement floored and lined at first only with hessian. There was a large "splat"-shaped stain on this same hessian, mute testimony to an uncharacteristic fit of rebellion against semolina for breakfast every morning by Margaret, and who could blame her? She and Bob were recovering from measles at the time and the heaped spoonful of semolina hit the wall in a most spectacular and satisfying manner as Mother disappeared around the verandah, kitchen bound. In a flurry of remorse and feverish giggles, the offending breakfast was scraped up before sliding far down the hessian lining and Mother, to our knowledge, never noticed. Or perhaps she just never enquired.

No description of home could be complete without mention of outbuildings, or, in the case of the laundry, lack of one. Two large galvanised iron tubs stood side by side on a plank supported by assorted bricks and props under the gum trees and this arrangement, with the nearby copper, was it. Open air washdays could be really pleasant, weather allowing, which was just as well as there was no alternative, and they often took on the bustle and atmosphere of some outlandish social occasion. Dad filled the tubs and copper and had kerosene buckets of clean water standing by for replenishment before he went out on his day's work. Cold ashes were raked out and the copper fire was lit and stoked with great hunks of wood that stuck several feet out of the fire-box, Dad never being one to do things in a faint hearted manner. There was a marvellous smell of burning gum leaves in the air and everyone who was available and old enough, helped where they could. I remember being given a blunt old knife for the job of cutting up chunks of yellow Signal Soap to put in the copper, as this was before the advent of packaged soap powders. Mother used a glass panelled washboard on which she scrubbed some of the more obstinately dirty articles and everything that could be boiled was. Sundry cats, dogs and pet lambs wandered about amongst the piles of sorted clothes or snoozed in the shade while a number of curious chooks came by to cast a critical eye over this weekly phenomenon, staying to squat in the heaps of cold ashes and ruffle them through their feathers. Anyone on their way through to the house paused long enough for a chat and to see how things were coming along.

But there were drawbacks. Gum nuts from overhanging trees dropped continually into tubs and copper and, on more than one occasion, a cow mooching past stopped to guzzle the water in which Mother had set clothes to soak overnight; steeping she called it. Morning saw the clothes high and dry and liberally marked with bits of chewed grass and green slaver! Poor Mother, she fought a continuous and losing battle with all the livestock about the place as the home block was inadequately fenced to say the least. But perhaps the greatest washday calamity of all was when Dad, helping out with enthusiasm and vigorous good intentions if nothing else, boiled two of Granny's good crepe dresses in a copper packed willy-nilly with everything else he could jam into it. The result was a couple of mud-coloured, tortured-looking crepe dresses, puckered and shrunken to grotesque and comic proportions while their copper mates, towels, shirts, and working-clothes were doomed to bear leprous pink and green blotches to the end of their natural life!

In fact, through her belongings, Granny was several times somewhat of an unwitting washday tragedy queen. One day one of the bull calves was feeling his oats and capering about near the long clothes line that stretched across the creek, caught his horns in a pair of Granny's best-quality "unmentionables". At first he tried playfully to back off but they were made of sturdy stuff and were quite firmly attached to his short horns. With a great lunge forward, away flew the two wooden pegs and with them, the long props used to help support the heavy lineful of wet clothes. Down came the line, trailing half the clothes in the sandy creek bed and off went the youngster, bawling with alarm and at intervals burrowing his head into the mud and sand, trying frantically to rid himself of this strange attachment. The last we saw of him that morning was as he frisked and burrowed off up the creek with Granny's ragged pennant slung rakishly over one eye. Granny, in true Victorian character, and no doubt still rankling from our shouts of indelicate laughter, was not amused. She firmly declined any of our conciliatory offers to go up the creek to look for the pants and I assume that the next time it flowed after rain, all evidence was washed discreetly away as we never found them while playing there.

At the end of a normal morning's proceedings, the copper was refilled with clean water and the fire stoked and kept going for the weekly evening baths which were taken with due ceremony in one of the galvanised tubs.

On cool evenings, the clothes horse was draped with sheets and blankets and positioned around the tub in front of the stove, to ensure as much privacy as was possible in a home where the kitchen was the nerve centre of our daily life. In summer, ablutions were performed in a small bough shed near the house which served as a bathroom in those early days, but which in time was replaced by a bathroom of sorts built onto the house. As for the washing, there was never enough space on the long line over the creek or the shorter one between two gum trees near the copper, so socks were strung out over a portion of fence and working clothes dangled over low tree branches. The place looked for all the world like some weird bazaar with queer and exotic fruits set out to dry in the sun.

The archaic pit-style dub stood some distance from the house on the bank of Ego Creek. Lofty and narrow and with a steeply-pointed red iron roof, it had adopted a slight tilt over the years which suggested a venerable, listening attitude. A magnificent spider orchid flowered year after year at the foot of one of the trees near the dub and we looked for it with the coming of spring every year on our daily "nature walks". A visit to this "convenience", which by its very nature I feel should be placed in inverted commas, could entail quite an expedition as one had to negotiate a thicket of giant sunflowers, climb through a wire fence, then follow a twisting sand track before arriving. There weren't many visitors to the farm in those days but if the need arose, imagine their embarrassment as, whilst trying to be as inconspicuous as possible, at least one curious dog, a cat or two and several highly vocal pet lambs joined the convoy!

The walls of the dub were, like the kitchen, unlined and white-washed and afflicted with a proportionate number of nail holes and on a leisurely evening visit, especially when it coincided with the washing-up, it was fun to line up an eye and squint through to see the first stars of the evening appear. Squares of torn up newspaper hung from a nail on the wall and there was a small pile of papers and periodicals on the floor, most of them with a farming accent. I remember sometimes seeking out "Tim Tyler's Luck" in the Western Mail to follow the escapades of Tim and his off-sider, Spud Murphy, and to look at their horses, one of which I seem to remember was called Rebel. The wooden seat of the dub was polished from use to the texture of marble and spiders inhabited the old building in multitudes. Red-backs nested at every vantage point and it must have been only good luck that none of us were ever bitten.

But what we kids feared most with a morbid dread, were the great hairy-legged spiders we called tarantulas or "trannies", that sprawled so menacingly on posts and walls. Being in a confined area, one couldn't retreat far if confronted and any sudden movement could mean contact, or worse still, send the creature scuttling up the wall to drop down into one's hair! Though it never happened, with imagination the possibilities were endless and nightmarish. Margaret was the only one of we females who wasn't scared of the trannies; she who seemed to bear malice to no living thing. So when one of us galloped back to the house shrieking, "Mother! Mother, there's a tranny in the dub!" if Margaret was around, she'd spare Mother who loathed the things as much as we did and come and shoosh the "poor old boy" outside, refusing to kill it as "he'd never done us any harm".

Night visits had special perils for we lesser mortals; not that we ever made the full journey at night unless absolutely necessary. For less than "absolutely necessary" reasons the big wattle tree by the wire fence was a perfectly adequate stopping off place and after the last lamp or candle was puffed out, there was a stout chamber pot in the marble-topped cupboard at the end of the sleepout for emergencies during the night. But when one did "have to go", it was necessary to carry a lamp or candle and it wasn't always easy to persuade someone to come for company, especially if the night looked particularly spooky. Once there, imagination ran riot as the branch of an overhanging tree scraped and tapped relentlessly on the iron roof and a vision of trannies lurking undetected in the flickering light, built up to panic proportions. The trip home was a stampede! The companion, waiting restively outside, was off like a shot at the first opportunity with shrieks of "Wait for me! Wait for me!" from the bearer of the light ringing in his ears as that poor individual wrestled with pyjama cords and pants and strove to keep up in spite of the handicap. Slippers were left to lie where they flew off, the candle flame extinguished itself as it fell in the sand and the wire fence was taken in a bound. We thrashed through the sunflowers like small tornadoes and skidded wildly as we hit the cement verandah before composing ourselves to re-enter the family scene as if nothing had ever been amiss.

* * *

There's not much of the old house left now, just the brick chimney that Jenny and I used to bounce our balls against and part of the verandah floor. The twisty gum corner posts, riddled by white ants, have long since collapsed and the walls, dangerously unstable, were of necessity demolished. I guess even at its best it must have looked a frightful old dump to a stranger's critical eye, but to us it was home and we loved it unashamedly.

Dad and Mother (the little one) before their marriage, with Daphne Davies and Dad's cousin Dorothy Whitfield.

CHAPTER 2

Without a doubt, Dad was the hero of our youth. As a tiny girl Margaret summed up our feelings for him when once, after pondering on the war he'd so vaguely heard about, Bob solemnly asked, "Why didn't the Germans catch you, Dad?" Margaret replied with withering scorn, "Don't be silly, Bob. The Germans couldn't run as fast as Dad!" It was enough to conjure up a picture of our Dad fleeing for his life with the might of the entire German army in hot pursuit! And years later when the second war moved closer and there was talk of evacuation, I can clearly remember thinking, "Well, we needn't worry. We've got Dad to look after us." He seemed so much taller and stronger and in every way more admirable than anyone else's Dad, but for all that he could be a very hard and exacting task master impatient, impulsive, never one to suffer fools gladly and gifted with a flair for picturesque dialogue in times of stress. We all had to bog in and do our share of the work, especially the older two and many a long day was spent in the sheepyard, chaff cutting, mustering or helping with lamb tailing. This was apart from the gentler pursuits of milking cows, feeding lambs, looking after chooks and all the other jobs that went with farming.

Dad hadn't had much schooling - four years he claimed - but he read many books on many and varied subjects and was careful to the point of being meticulous in his choice of words either written or spoken. For years there was a slim volume of Adam Lindsay Gordon's poetry on the shelf, from which he loved to quote, particularly from "The Sick Stockrider". He took a keen interest in national and world affairs, was a devout supporter of R.G. Menzies and later in life, even sent a cable to one of the United States Presidents advising on how to deal with some international crisis he felt strongly about.

If Dad was our hero, Mother was a modest little heroine. How she would have protested at the term or the very idea of it, but in her quiet little way, she was one. Not that she did anything dramatic like going overland behind cattle or going far off the beaten track at all. As Dad used to say himself, her strength lay in the fact that, when it would have been so much easier to let things go and forget standards from the past, she never did, but retained them under the most trying conditions. There was a time and a place for everything, a right way to do things and the important thing was to "make the effort".

As a small child, under school age, I can remember Mother baking the bread in the afternoon, first kneading the dough in a big china bowl and putting it in the oven before having a brief "lie down". After this, it was time to wash and change. There was no question of a daily bath or shower at this stage as water had to be carted and as for hair washing, that took on the pro-portions of a major undertaking with dippers of precious rainwater being portioned out and handled with infinite care to avoid spillage. For her wash, Mother would carry some water to the small bathroom and after this, there'd be a clean change before doing her hair. I loved to sit on the wide bed and watch her at the dressing table brushing her hair before doing it up into a soft bun on the nape of her neck. A light dusting of face powder and a nightly application of cold cream, year in year out, were her only beauty aids. The faint perfume of powder and cold cream is forever associated in my mind with Mother's dressing table.

With Mother in our Sunday best. Note Bob's tie and bare feet!

Outings were as infrequent as visitors then and Mother said once that she didn't get off the place for seven months though we were only ten miles from town. This was no doubt why so much importance was attached to Sunday afternoon tea; it was our weekly "social" occasion. All we children were rounded up, washed and changed - Margaret, Jenny and I with ribbons on our protesting heads and Bob reluctantly sporting a tie. Quite often his feet were bare but the tie was firmly "in situ". David, three years my junior, would have been at this stage, a baby in the big cane pram.

Usually we'd have it at the big oval table in what was rather grandly called the dining room or, on hot days, out on the verandah shaded by creeper. A starched white cloth covered the table and when no-one was looking, Jenny and I made faces at ourselves in the silver tea-pot which was polished to brilliance and earned ourselves a sharp rebuke from Grandpa for giggling. There were glass cups and saucers that had been the reward of careful saving of the ends of certain tea packets, and the fare was simple - rock cakes or scones or, if the hens were laying well, a sponge cake or maybe just bread and butter, cut as thinly as possible, and plenty of tea for all. Occasionally we'd have visitors from town, an aunt and uncle and three cousins and on these days the conversation would take on a slightly broader aspect with news from town, but otherwise it must have been far from scintillating - the weather, the stock and crops and bits of news gathered from papers, and so on. But the effort was made and that was what mattered.

Afterwards, on the days without our cousins, Mother would take us for a walk and generally, by popular vote, we'd head off up the Mail Gate Road that ran alongside the creek to the mailbox on the main road. Sometimes we looked for mushrooms or wildflowers or the gum that ran down the trunks of some wattle trees and made glue when heated. Often the knobs of gum were quite chewable with a hard, tough skin on the outside and a soft, almost liquid centre. Mother sometimes gathered some of the brownish red gumtips that substituted for flowers and looked attractive in a pair of old brass vases standing on a china cupboard in the dining room; and other times we just walked. There was a smell about the creek, more pronounced in summer than winter: the smell of salt and mud and ti-tree and sheep. Flanked by wattles and scrubby cockatoo bush and full of paperbarked ti-trees, it meandered right past the house and horse yards and was a wonderful place to play or hide out in when in trouble. Stock watered at the permanent brackish waterholes and licked the salt that crystallised on the surrounding sand. On still evenings, frogs plonk-plonked ceaselessly amongst the bullrushes near the water and the quaint, muffled cry of the mopoke sounded faintly eerie as we lay in our beds in the long sleepout.

According to Grandpa, who had lived most of his life in the area, the name Ego meant "snake" in the native dialect, but we never gave it a thought in the many hours we spent engrossed in catching tadpoles in the shallow, sandy rivulets or building cubby houses of the fallen brush and timber. There were trees too, with branches bent at just the right angle for "riding" and on these imaginary steeds we rode for miles and hours, using bits of bagging for saddles and bindertwine for stirrups. Invariably a game would start off with a decision to, "Say we're poor . . .". It sounded so romantic and such exciting things happened to poor children - in fact they seemed to end up having all the fun if stories could be believed. Goodness, if only we d known, there was no need to pretend, but we were blissfully unaware. Later, when experimenting with smoking, the creek was a haven in which to puff and gasp at our abominable concoctions of dried cockatoo bush flower and old tea leaves rolled up in newspaper!

Various types of spider and donkey orchids and small purple pom-poms, papery everlastings and kangaroo paws grew along the creek banks. In March every year, "adjigo", a native creeper, with its small, yellow flower spread frail tendrils and clung to anything that would support it. Grandpa said the tuber of the plant was good to eat and tasted like sweet potato, though we never tried it. Further down, near the boundary fence, the creek ran out onto a flat, marshy patch that was overgrown with a tall, rank weed we called "stinking Roger". If a cow grabbed more than a mouthful of it in passing, the milk tasted accordingly.

Clouds of pink and grey galahs descended in screeching hordes on the big gum trees in the creek as it twisted past the horseyards, attracted by the fallen grain from mangers and nosebags. But best of all we loved to hear the black cockatoos or "will-yarks" as we called them because of the strange, wild, whimpering cry they uttered as they wheeled overhead - "will-yark! will-yark!" Like the strings of processional caterpillars and the whippy streaks of white cloud Grandpa called "mares' tails", they were conceded to be a sign of rain and were often doubly welcome.

For all these reasons we invariably chose the creek as the venue for our Sunday afternoon walks and we'd set off like the bush mother and her family in Henry Lawson's "The Drover's Wife", with Mother pushing the old pram and the rest of us keeping our own pace. Mother often took a book to read to us, finding a fallen log to sit on once we'd walked a while or maybe she'd take some sewing or darning, making good use of the daylight as the kerosene lamps in the house left much to be desired. One small, ginger teddy bear took on a decidedly malevolent expression after having bright pink buttons sewn on for eyes, mistaken in the poor light for brown!

On the other side of the creek we'd pass the spot where Jack and Liza, an elderly aboriginal couple had camped while working on the place. Liza had doted on Jenny as a toddler, Mother said, fascinated by her fair skin and hair, sitting cross-legged in the shade for hours to play with her. Liza must also have been a past master at understatement according to Mother. On the rare occasions that visitors came to the house in those days, every dog snoozing and dozing on the verandah or under the trees, would be galvanised into action, whoofing and bounding out to meet this unexpected intrusion on their privacy. At such times, Liza would be moved to comment to Mother, "Mide be someone come, Missus. Dawg swingin 'is tail!" Theirs must have been an illegal union according to Liza's own conscience as once she complained to Mother she was "berry, berry tired, Missus". Mother told her to go and lie down for a while and have a little sleep. But Liza rolled her eyes at the suggestion, glancing fearfully over her shoulder and said in a hoarse whisper, "No Missus. No lie down. Mide be someone choke'm!" Poor spindle-shanked, sad-eyed old Jack seemed only moderate compensation for so constant and sleepless a vigil against such drastic reprisal!

Bob had a cubby by the creek too when he was a bit older, an underground cubby dug painstakingly out in a patch of soft yellow sand by a grove of small pine trees. Small sisters were definitely out of bounds but I must have made it at least once as I can still remember the steps and shelves carved out of the cool sand, an improvised fireplace and the bamboo thatching that reinforced the roof. It was the combination of these last two factors that caused a near disaster. One afternoon, flames from the fire on which he was roasting potatoes and onions, caught the dry thatching and quickly spread to nearby grass. There was a spectacular blaze as it moved amongst fallen timber and dried pine cones and went on to burn out part of the cow paddock before being belted out with green branches and wet bags. Providentially, Bob had managed to scramble out before the roof caved in, but it was the end of the cool, private little retreat he'd toiled with such energy and imagination to perfect.

Further up the creek, towards the mail gate, there was a section where some type of vine grew thickly over low ti-tree bushes, forming a kind of springy matting. As older kids, Jenny, David and I would disappear up the creek and spend hours clambering, springing and bouncing on the vines, using them much as children do a trampoline. How we never staked ourselves on broken and jagged branches protruding through the matting I'll never know. It just seemed there must have been a guardian angel looking after us all the time when I think back. We were fortunate not to have had more encounters with snakes than we did in all our barefoot, carefree hours, but I really don't remember many, or in fact taking many precautions to avoid them in spite of Mother's warnings.

By now the afternoon shadows would be drawing out and we were each in our own little world of thought as we mooched down the road to home; Margaret and Bob to change out of their good clothes and get the cows in for milking and Jenny and I to help Grandpa feed the chooks and collect the eggs. It wouldn't go down very well now as Sunday afternoon entertainment but we knew no alternative and although we'd seen and done nothing new, it was an outing and we'd look forward to doing it all again next Sunday.

CHAPTER 3

Joshua Mills, Dad's father, lived with us for many years and, during this time, must often have been a trial to Mother's already heavily taxed patience with his old man's crustiness. But she also had in him a staunch ally in some matters. One piece of advice he gave her early in her farm life was, "Now my girl, don't you learn to milk that cow!" And she never did. Grandpa wasn't a talker or a yarn spinner. Most of what he said was delivered in staccato bursts and in old age at least, all his predictions were gloomy. Whenever we ran about on the verandah where he sat in the sun, we were "up to monkey tricks" and doomed to "bark your shins!" Ice cream as well as the creeper I've mentioned, was "full of rats!" which didn't worry us as we never had it then anyway. Apparently, from what Mother could gather, on one of his rare ventures into an ice cream parlour, he'd spied a rat in the rafters as he was enjoying his dish of ice cream and the association of ideas stayed with him from that day on. Rabbit was not fit for human consumption as it was classified "vermin" by the Road Board and no amount of preparation on Mother's part would persuade him to touch it.

Once Mother was taking us to a Sunday School picnic by the river on a nearby property and from the start things went wrong, as though Fate was determined to hinder us. The buggy mare was unusually frisky and refused to be caught. Instead of standing still and acting like a lady, she frisked her tail as she careered about the dam paddock, kicking up her heels and making the noises that only a well fed buggy mare can make. At last, with all hands out, she was cornered, caught and harnessed. Then the reins were missing Dad had taken them up on the hill with the team. So Wendy the pony was caught and Bob was sent off, fill tilt, to get them. After sundry other hold-ups, we climbed aboard the stylish buggy with four high wheels that we used for such outings, with Margaret taking the reins as usual. Grandpa hobbled out to see us off, leaning heavily on his stick as he eyed the buggy.

"Well, my girl," he said to Mother in his curiously staccato manner, "I hope you get there without that back wheel coming off!" Mother said if she'd had something large and heavy in her hands at that moment, she would have been sorely tempted to lean over and dong him on the head with it after all the trials they'd had.

Perhaps some pessimism was ingrained into these hardy old bush folk as a safety valve against some of the calamities that did overtake them in reality. After all, his first child, a girl, lived only a few days and later his wife died from haemorrhage following a miscarriage when my father was ten and his sister, Betty, slightly younger. An old sepia-coloured photograph shows Grandmother Mills as a bonny, dark-eyed young woman before her marriage when she was Hannah Maley, one of the fourteen children of John Stephen Maley and his wife, Elizabeth, formerly Elizabeth Kniest Waldeck. Their homestead, originally known as Home Cottage, is now a folk museum on the wind-swept Greenough Flats, just south of Geraldton.

I must find out more about Hannah; the little picture intrigues me, with her direct, dark gaze and back so straight. One of the few things I can recall Dad telling us about her was of the time when they were at a lonely station where Grandpa was manager. More often than not he was away from the homestead out on the run, and she was there alone with the two small children. The day that stuck in Dad's memory, not surprisingly, was when wild bush natives surrounded the house, spears in hand and of how his mother went out, erect and unarmed, to parley with them. One can imagine the young woman with the terrified little boy clinging to her skirt and the baby asleep in the house behind, surrounded by jabbering, muttering wild men, negotiating on some grievance, more than likely at least partly in their own language, until they reluctantly dispersed, going back to the bush.

Speaking of old timers and their pessimism though, perhaps the ultimate was manifested in one of our elderly neighbours who always had a clean white sheet in the cupboard in the perpetual expectation that her husband would drop dead. Ironically, she pre-deceased him by many years!

Grandpa had been born on Narra Tarra, not far from our place, in eighteen fifty-nine and could remember the days when sailing ships came into the bay. I wish now that he'd told us more and we'd listened with more attention to what he did say: there must have been so much to hear about the early days of the colony when his own father, John Mills, was a mounted trooper before developing the Narra Tarra estate. One thing I do remember him telling us about was how, as a boy, he rode daily to the top of a hill on what was later to be our place, to look out over the sea for the sailing ship bringing his mother back after a visit to Perth. There was no other way to let the family know or send a message of any kind and one can imagine the slender boy astride his horse on the windy hill, straining his eyes to the far horizon for the first sight of sail that would start him riding full tilt the several miles to home to tell the news and send a buggy rattling off along the rough bush track to meet her. I wonder how many times he rode home disappointed after being met only by the wind and the blank, blue sky before that happy day. Now a tall television tower stands on that same hill, on the way to where he would have ridden.

During his long life in the bush, Grandpa had been a Government stock inspector at a time when some kind of scab was rife amongst the sheep population, and had at different times managed Barnong and Gabyon stations in the Murchison district. Later he'd been an inspector for one of the banks, travelling a vast area from Yuna to almost as far south as Moora. His method of operation was to put his buggy and pair of ponies on the train, to be off loaded at a central point, driving about from there to check on improvements such as fencing, clearing and water supplies. For many years he was a Justice of the Peace in Geraldton, a Member of Parliament for not so many, and a judge of ring events at all the country shows around the Geraldton area in the days when ladies rode side-saddle and gentlemen drove four-in-hands.

Sometimes, in his more mellow moods, Grandpa would read to us. "Jasper Jay and the Seventeen Sunflowers" was a great favourite but for some reason of his own, he simply refused to read another story from the same book, "Poor Porkette". It was, from memory, the tale of a small, spotted pig going to market, getting lost and ending up happily at home after a series of unlikely adventures.

Walking with Grandpa — Enga, Margaret and Jenny.

We must have done it to death - or maybe we always cried over it, but eventually he'd agree to read us "anything but 'Poor Porkette'. No, no, no! I won't read 'Poor Porkette!'"

Before our first radio set arrived, we had only a derelict gramophone with a remarkably limited selection of records. The ones played most were "The Whistler and His Dog", something that sounded like "Your Boys are Ringing My Silver Bell", "Barnacle Bill the Sailor" and, when Grandpa was thought to be out of earshot, "Hallelujah, I'm a Bum" - not because it was particularly musically favoured, but because he disapproved of it so heartily we felt there must have been more to it than met the ear. Whenever he heard it he'd tut-tut rapidly and say to Mother, "Hallelujah, I'm a Bum. Bum indeed! Can't understand Stuart bringing such a thing into the house with young children about!" He simply couldn't see that there was or could be a meaning to the offending word other than the one obvious to him and it offended him mightily.

Up to the very last years of his life, Grandpa continued to drive about the farm with his elderly bay mare, Minnie, in the shafts. He was a great old stockman and there were always fences, dams and sheep to check on. As a small child, while the "others" were at school, I often went with him on these excursions, sitting on the floor of the buggy and watching fascinated over the dashboard as, mile after mile, Minnie's shod hooves crunched over the rough ground, her hind legs shooting backwards and forwards like pistons from my privileged viewpoint. We'd rattle on for ages, sometimes with Grandpa deep in thought and nothing but the rumble and crunch of iron tyred wheels and the mare's hoofbeats to accompany us. At other times he'd sing to me in his croaky, old man's voice - something with a horsey flavour; like the little song I remember, "Horsey, keep your tail up and keep the sun out of my eyes". It didn't make much sense but it was an effort for him and we enjoyed it. Grandpa had strange names for some things too; native names many of them. Banksias he called what sounded like "mungites", though I've never heard the term used by anyone else. I remember him saying that snake, cooked in the ashes was delicious and tasted like fish and thinking that it was funny how he could have eaten snake, probably as a boy with his native childhood companions, but refused to have anything to do with rabbit which to me was quite acceptable. He was a pious old man and told me snatches from the Bible in his jerky manner, always from the Old Testament and one day I brought down on my own head his full wrath by calling one of the dogs, probably his beloved Mate, a sod. I'd heard the term and thought I was being very clever to apply it appropriately, but Grandpa was horrified, not surprisingly, that a small girl should have heard, let alone used such language and I imagine Dad had to account for it when we arrived home.

In lean seasons, Grandpa would give a hand by feeding the sheep and on these days we'd go out in the buggy with a couple of bags of "fodder" as he called it on the floor, behind the seat. And there was one day that didn't have such a happy ending for me. We had on board a bag or two of Meggitt's Nuts, a concentrated stock food with what must have been a high content of linseed oil. It was warm this particular day and the charm of Minnie's flashing hooves at last lost out against the enticingly nutty smell issuing from the bag in the back of the buggy. Small, persistent fingers soon worked an opening between the stitching in the top of the bag and the first nibble was rewardingly delicious. Grandpa would have been preoccupied with his own thoughts and quite oblivious to my mischief so one nut followed another until, alas, it was too late. Overcome by heat, the constant rocking of the buggy, the smell of sweating horse and plain over-indulgence in something never intended for human consumption anyway, I realised my folly. By the time we arrived home, I was lolling wretchedly on the buggy floor, pea-green with biliousness, Mother told me later, and reeking of linseed oil. It's still one of my least favourite smells.

* * *

Granny Mountain, our maternal grandmother, lived in Geraldton until the early war years when she came to live with us for a time. In town she shared a house with one of her elderly, widowed friends and we relished the rare occasions when we could visit her. Generally there was something in the ice box just a little different to what we had at home - the ice box itself was a novelty to us - and her pastries and pie crusts were something to be dreamed of. A small lady with very white hair and a chuckling laugh, she was an ardent devotee to her weekly game of croquet, walking several miles each way to the green. Granny's clothes always smelt of lavender from the small "lavender ladies" she tucked away in her drawers between the layers of clothes and hung in corners of her wardrobe and to me she was the original Lavender Lady herself when I was small.

Granny had an adage or philosophy to suit every occasion and condition of mankind and "This too shall pass", must have helped her over many of the crises in her own life; there must have been many as by the time she died in her ninety-fourth year, she was survived by only three of her eight children. Originally from Queensland, she told us sometimes of how as a girl, she'd ridden sidesaddle on her bay mare, galloping with her sisters on her father's property and I had a mental picture of a laughing child with long, fair hair blowing in the wind and streaming out behind her as she rode. At nineteen she'd married a man nearly twice her age and followed him to the various places where he was employed by Burns Philp and Company. Mother and her older brother, Torres, were both born on Thursday Island. After moving to Geraldton, Grandpa Mountain had his own business as a wine and spirit merchant and general provider.

Mother told us that Granny was born the seventh child of a seventh child and, believe it if you will, perhaps this accounts in part for the strange experience she once had. Granny never mentioned it to us, in fact it had been years before she'd mentioned it to her husband as she no doubt felt she'd have been scoffed at as a silly young thing with too much imagination. This is how Mother related the episode as told to her, without embellishment. At the time they were living at a big old house in Geraldton and Grandpa, of necessity, was quite often away overnight on business. This particular evening, Granny was sitting up late, sewing by lamplight. The three young children were all asleep in bed and the house was still and quiet. At last, making a move to pack things away for the night, something caused her to glance up and she was astonished to see an old man with a long white beard sitting in a chair near the closed door. He was leaning forward slightly, with his chin resting on his hands, supported by a walking stick. His steady gaze was kindly and without a trace of malice or mischief.

She rubbed her eyes and thought, "It's only the lamp casting shadows. There can't be anyone. The door's locked!" But when she looked again, he was still there, fixing her with a steady gaze and just the hint of a smile, his dark eyes unwavering. By now she was alarmed and jumped up to break the spell that the quietness had cast. When she dared to look again he'd gone, leaving no trace but her pounding heart. Many years later she'd mentioned the incident to Grandpa Mills, who listened with surprising attention and interest. After brief reflection on her description of the long white beard, dark eyes and hawk-like features, he told her, "That would have been old Costello. You need never have been afraid of him. Costello never hurt anyone." He told her too that the old man had been a ticket-of-leave man, and had worked as an ostler at the nearby hotel. He had died under mysterious circumstances and his body had been found floating in the sea. An enquiry had done nothing to solve the riddle and the case was closed.

* * *

Certainly, on reflection, perhaps there was just a "touch of the fey" about Granny Mountain. Often her instincts were right, "feelings" she called them, and never more so than on the night before she died in a Perth nursing home. She was a favourite with the staff and this night when the young nurse called in to settle her and bid her a cheery "Goodnight, Mrs. Mountain. See you in the morning", the old lady replied quite firmly but without a trace of drama or self-pity, "No, dear. I won't be here in the morning". And she wasn't.

CHAPTER 4

Country children had to be pretty resourceful and determined to manage a treat they particularly wanted then and Margaret and Bob were no exception when they set their hearts on seeing the picture "Tom Sawyer" which was coming to town. They'd both read the book and pleaded most eloquently to be allowed to see it. There was no question of everyone going so Dad arranged for one of our neighbours to pick them up and drop them off at the mail box on the main road after the show. The day arrived after what seemed to them like an eternity of waiting and, that evening after an early tea, Dad drove them up in the buggy to wait for Mr. Webber and his truck. Everything went as planned and the picture was everything they could have wanted and expected. Every moment was recalled and relived as they bumped happily along beside Mr. Webber on the trip home.

He waited with them while they lit their smoky kerosene lantern at the gate and, after a cheerful reassurance that they'd be "quite all right now", he left them to the mile-long walk home beside the creek, as planned. The stillness of the night wrapped around them as the lights of the truck disappeared over the rise and the companionable sound of the engine died away. For a few moments they walked in silence, the lantern flame a pinprick of light in the dark. Then, "It was good wasn't it?"

"Yeah !" Silence again as they plodded on.

"What about the part in the cave. Spooky, wasn't it?" "I'll say!" The lantern bobbed with every footstep and the silence was intense. "Come on, Bob. Can't you walk a bit faster?"

"All right. I'm going as fast as I can." He managed to manfully lengthen his stride to keep up with Margaret's longer one but his busy mind was still pondering the details of what they had just seen.

"What about the part where...?"

"Don't talk now Bob, let's get home first." And so they strode on, the lantern flame quivering between them. Then: "Ssshhh! What was that?"

"What? I didn't hear anything!" "Listen!" They stood stock still, straining their ears into the night, afraid of what they might hear. Suddenly the familiar tree-lined creek had taken on a remarkably sinister blackness and instinctively they huddled closer together. Yes. There was something: a muffled, regular beat and a faint, faint jingling sound. It seemed to be coming closer even as they listened. "What is it?" Bob croaked, his throat suddenly dry.

"I dunno but it sounds like something coming." They swallowed hard and listened again, with hearts bumping like scared rabbits. They weren't half way home yet. Could they run for it or should they hide until "it" had gone? What if ...? "What are we going to do?"

"Put the lantern out, then they mightn't see us." Trembling fingers pressed the lever to lift the glass and the little flame was puffed out. The beat came closer. Half-paralysed with fright, the two kids headed for the nearest bush and huddled behind it, hardly daring to breathe. "Do you think they saw us?" "I dunno. Ssshhh ..." Then, horror or horrors! A faint light that seemed to bob and weave and swing about could be seen dimly through the trees. Could it be a phantom light? Or maybe someone running? But who at this time of night? There was talk every now and then of phantom lights over near the Greenough Flats and everyone had heard of the Bootenal lights - not that they'd ever believed those tales anyway, but ... They couldn't have run now if they'd had to; the hammering of their hearts was almost suffocating. There was nothing to do but crouch as small as possible and wait for that awful beating, jingling, bobbing light to pass them by. That's if it did... They waited; mesmerised.

An eternity later a large, dark shape rounded the bend in the track and loomed out of the night as Mr. Gatsos, one of the Macedonian tomato gardeners from nearby, and his trusty black nag, Shaky, hove into view - a hurricane lantern swinging eerily under the cart! The dreaded beat had been the rhythmical steady pounding of Shaky's large hooves as he trotted thankfully in the direction of home, his harness jingling companionably.

Too stunned at first to grasp the truth, the kids stayed where they were, weak with mingled fright and relief.

'It's only Mr. Gatsos!" "Yeah !"

"Let's ask him for a ride. I want to get home!" So they stood up and stumbled out to hail the astonished traveller who was returning home late from town, via the short cut, and certainly not expecting to see anyone else abroad at that time of night. Shaky, thoroughly alarmed at the dramatic appearance of these two wraith-like figures from behind a perfectly ordinary-looking bush, swerved violently, almost unseating his driver from the spartan plank that served as a seat in the cart.

"It's only us, Mr. Gatsos." The call was meant to be reassuring, but the outline in the cart looked far from reassured as he peered into the night, unsure whether to stay or let Shaky have his head and make for home!

"It's us, Mr. Gatsos, Margaret and Bob. Can we have a ride home please?"

And so at last Shaky was reined in hard, snorting reproachfully at this unscheduled delay, as the children scrambled thankfully into the cart. They completed their journey in style but many times relived the fright of that night, each time with more embellishment than the last and I wouldn't mind betting their co-traveller had more of a fright than he'd care to admit that dark night too.

* * *

Margaret and Bob were still only a pair of kids when they and Francis, one of Bob's friends from down the road, had a memorable jaunt to get the mail which was dropped off twice weekly by the Yuna Mail truck. The boys had decided to put their budding mechanical instincts to use on a derelict buggy that stood slowly deteriorating under the gum trees by the horse yards. All the morning they had toiled manfully on its renovation with spanners and screwdrivers and pots of axle grease, until they were satisfied it was a going concern. Dad cast an eye over their work and at last agreed to let them use it on the mail run, as long as they used the quietest of the buggy horses. So Minnie, Grandpa's mare was caught and harnessed.

At this point a furious row developed about who was to drive. Margaret declared that, as the oldest, it was her right, while Bob demanded to know who'd done all the work on the buggy anyway, and anyway, she always drove! The work argument applied to Francis too and there couldn't be two drivers so Dad stepped in to arbitrate and at last they started with Margaret driving and a glowering "mechanic" on either side. At first the wheels rolled sweetly and tempers cooled with the pleasure and achievement of it all.

After a while though, it felt as though all was not quite right and they knocked and grated along until Bob noticed that the right hand back wheel was winding its way almost off the axle. They all gingerly alighted, Margaret holding the mare's head while the boys lifted and puffed and pushed and worked the wheel back on again. All aboard and off they started, but soon it was the left wheel that gave trouble. The performance was repeated and after a few such interruptions, they decided it would be easier and safer if the boys walked, one on either side to shout "Stop!" whenever necessary. So, for the rest of the journey, Margaret rode in solitary splendour, looking like the Queen of Sheba, with a thoroughly disgruntled footman plodding on either side.

A half hour trip took on two hour proportions and Dad was setting off to walk up the road to look for them when at last they wobbled into view. After that, the old buggy was retired back to the trees. We kids spent hours playing in it, imagining it was a covered wagon or a Cobb and Co. coach, numerous kittens were born under its seat and some of the more adventurous hens made their nests in it, so it was useful to the last.

* * *

It must have been because of the outdoor, active life we lived, that we were always "starving" at meal times. Mother was a very good plain cook and turned out marvellous meals from her array of heavy, black cast-iron pots and meat boilers and enamel saucepans that sprouted "pot mends" like a whiskery chin. Nothing was wasted and because we were always hungry, there was no need to enforce the rule of "eat it up or go without". There was no alternative anyway. And so, as well as stews and roasts and boiled mutton, we cleaned up liver and heart, brains and tongue, sheep's head soup and tough old hens and swede turnips by the sackful: and asked for more. Rabbit was the only alternative to mutton and the old hens, and while the rest of us enjoyed it, Grandpa and Bob refused it; Grandpa because of his aversion to "vermin", and Bob because it was his task to catch and skin the rabbits and he couldn't bring himself to eat them after that.

Fresh dripping was always a treat, especially when there was a good deposit of thick, salty "gravy" under the fat and before serving a roast, poor Mother had to ward us all off as we descended, each with a chunk of bread to dip into the baking dish. But the two things regarded as special treats in our diet at this stage were fresh fruit and "bought" butter. Both were hard to come by and, in the case of butter, stocking up was out of the question as we had no way to keep it. The stick Mother used to make our own salty, yellow variety was about fifteen inches long and of a hard black wood worn almost to the dimensions of a knife blade. She must have beaten her way patiently through tons of the stuff. So not only was shop butter appreciated for its texture and taste, but for Mother, the fact of not having had to make it added special appeal. In fact, one of the few times she was moved to tears of despair and disappointment was over the loss of a pound of butter.

Watermelon time on the verandah.

They'd come home one day after a trip to town in the buggy. Somehow she'd managed to keep the butter cool enough on the way home to stop it melting, and had turned it out onto a plate and set it on the kitchen table in the breeze while she attended to one of us. No-on gave a thought to Soda, the brindled kangaroo dog skulking on the side verandah. It was all over in a second. Unimpeded by fly-wire doors, Soda, with as much instinct as anyone else for the good things in life, entered stealthily and, rearing on his long hind legs, grasped the prize in his jaws, knocking the plate to the floor. Mother heard the plate smash and ran into the kitchen in time to see Soda making off, tail between his legs, to enjoy his ill-gained treat in private. He was never forgiven for that lapse from grace.

Another minor catastrophe centred around a bag of pears which was eagerly awaited and had at last arrived on the mail truck. Dad picked them up in the buggy and as soon as he arrived home, had unharnessed and tied up Peter, the little grey horse, and taken the mail inside, leaving the precious pears on the buggy seat. Once inside there was mail to read and papers to browse through over a cup of tea and so it was some time before he gave in to our pestering and stood up saying, 'Well, I'd better get those pears in, I suppose".

But Peter had been making good use of his time. It hadn't taken him long to find he had enough rope to investigate this delicious new aroma wafting from what looked strangely like a nosebag! The sight that met our eyes as we followed Dad in high anticipation, was a replete and contended horse and a sack, soggy with juice and bits of chewed pear, almost empty. He'd nipped and gobbled and slobbered his way through the whole lot, any remains being so contaminated by horsey breath and tooth marks as to be unusable. Our reproachfulness and disappointment were profound. The pears were to be such a treat and now they were gone. But there was nothing we could do about it and Peter was quite unperturbed by our heartfelt wishes for a good bellyache for his enterprise.

We did some bartering with the Macedonians for tomatoes and melons and other vegetables we didn't grow, mainly through lack of water, giving them in exchange meat, eggs, fresh dripping, milk or figs that grew on several big trees near the house - whatever we had that they could use. One little man would sometimes come to the house with a special gift for Mother, creaking up in his dilapidated spring cart, making all the dogs bark — a quaint, lonely little figure in ill-fitting clothes and with a decidedly dispirited droop to his bushman-style moustache. With infinite dignity, he'd bow from the waist, offering a fine melon or marrow and saying slowly, "For you, Meesus." We never did know his name and called him simply, "Mother's Little Man".

These people in their cluster of small, white houses set amongst the gardens, were part of our childhood scene and we accepted their presence without often wondering how they came to be in our out-of-the-way little corner of the world. Mother said they were probably refugees from some political upheaval in Europe during the nineteen twenties.

They worked hard and whole families toiled long hours in the gardens and makeshift packing sheds; grandmothers, young children and pregnant women alike. The older women in their unrelieved black dresses, thick stockings and heads swathed in babushkas, seemed watchful and suspicious at the approach of strangers and the houses smelt perpetually of soup and cabbage.

One of the things we children found most fascinating about these neighbours of ours were the curious and often irrelevant names they chose for their livestock. As well as Shaky, which was a singularly sturdy black gelding and not a bit as his name suggested, there was a placid brown cow called Chasy, and a bad-tempered dog named Paul. Old Louis, the Albanian, kept up a running patter to his bay mare, shaking a whip he never used and muttering, "Hurry up, Lala! Hurry up, Lala!" Lala never did hurry up, but plodded on, year in year out with her bottom lip drooping and arrived at wherever they were going in her own good time.

Louis was a dignified-looking old man, perhaps he wasn't even old, but to a child he seemed so. He carried himself very straight and always wore a black hat and dark navy blue suit, complete with waistcoat, no matter what the day. Whenever he took eggs home from us, he insisted that Mother hard boil them first, all of them, as apparently he didn't trust the springs of his cart to guarantee them a safe passage home in their natural state. I can just remember standing with Mother on the verandah as he solemnly tapped a random sample on the heel of his boot, testing before he set out on the journey home.

One day, our nearest neighbour, Mr. Raykos, called in on his way home to show us the fine pair of plough horses he'd just taken delivery of and had promptly named Mary and Roderick. He was so immensely proud of this fine looking pair and Dad had to admire them too, though he felt the latter may prove too much of a handful for his new owner. As it turned out, Mary was of an agreeable disposition, but from the beginning, spirited, highstepping Roderick made it quite clear he didn't see his destiny in pulling a plough for Mr. Raykos or anyone else, most likely. One afternoon, soon after their arrival, we guessed something was wrong by the shouts coming from the garden down near the dam.

Next minute out flew a bay horse, harnessed to a single furrow plough and, in hot pursuit, his agitated owner, running as fast as his short legs would allow, with clenched fists raised and whole being rigid with despair and rage. With every few steps he shouted after the fast disappearing horse, "Buddy busta! Buddy busta!". But Roderick cared not a jot. His head was up and his tail was up and he was off with the plough bucking and plunging behind him so that he was fortunate not to have his hind legs ploughed into the ground as he went.

One of our horses was tied up at the house, so Margaret was sent off, poste haste, to round up the runaway. It wasn't long before the load proved too much for Roderick at that speed and he came to a standstill, mouth agape and heaving sides white with foam. He was led home that night a chastened horse but with spirit undaunted. From then on mild Mary did the work and Roderick kept clear of anything that looked like a bridle or collar and grew fat and sleek amongst the melons and pumpkins.

CHAPTER 5

If there was a favourite time of the year for us, though every season was welcomed in turn, it would have been when the first of the winter rains came. One memory that will stay with me forever, is looking out across the Clover paddock from the verandah and seeing sheets of rain sweeping in from the northwest, blotting out the hills behind and the horses backing into it with their heads down and streaming tails flattened against their rumps.

How snug and secure we felt in our funny old house by the creek as rain thundered on the iron roof, drowning out all attempts at conversation, and cascaded under the outside door of the sleepout unless someone promptly jammed a rolled-up wheat bag against it. This was a time for hot cocoa and sitting around the kitchen stove at night while the wind tossed the branches on the big gum trees down by the copper until they roared like the sea. In bed we heard the joyful chorus of frogs in the creek as we huddled under our motley collections of bush rugs and dressing gowns and anything else we could lay hands on for extra warmth. After good rains, the old creek raged by, swollen to a muddy, red torrent, topped with piles of ginger foam that bobbed and swirled as it went and we kids could look forward to hours of tadpoling and paddling and just mucking about, squelching the soft red mud between our bare toes. This rain also signalled the start of seeding, and horses, harness and machinery were checked and ready to go.

We were all proud of Dad's team of work horses and they were certainly a handsome lot; eight powerful Clydesdales abreast, white blazed faces and hairy fetlocks nodding and plodding in unison. Dad considered the Clydesdale to be the best all-round "good doer" and they were generally placid and easy to handle by nature. Each one was named and seemed to have its own individual personality. There was sensible, hard-working bay Captain on the outside, Roman-nosed Reuben and huge, roan Baldy whose baleful wall eye gave him a strangely mean look when really he was the most even tempered and predictable of creatures. Pretty, fidgety Peggy was the only unsound body amongst them and Dad reckoned she had a weak heart. After a morning's work, she'd be trembling with fatigue and have to be replaced in the team by a spare at the dinnertime stop. There were always several of these led out each morning so that each horse had some time during a working week, resting up as a spare. Some of them I remember were big, grey Prince, old Potgut whose name spoke for itself, and smoky black Jerry. Back in the lineup, poor, mad Jack pitched himself into his collar as though his life depended on doing the job single-handed. And so on, with chestnut Caesar next to him, then bossy Kate, a great heavyweight of a mare and speckled Blossom on the far side.

We went out with Dad and the team whenever we were at home and he'd take us during seeding and oh! the thrill of being handed the reins as we stood beside him on the narrow plank of the Sunderseeder. With the heavy, sweet smell of freshly-turned earth, the twinge and creak of straining trace chains and whippletrees and salt-crusted reins slap-slapping on broad, sweating rumps, I used to dream of growing up to drive a team forever. The only jarring note on these idyllic days was the cry of the plovers as they swooped and fretted overhead, trying desperately and in vain to save their nests on the ground from the clomping hooves, the cutting discs of the machinery and the raking steel claws of the harrows that dragged behind.

Time for dinner was gauged roughly by the sun but mostly by the degree of hunger felt. This factor was often the cause of some very early lunches, or "dinner" as we never failed to call it, especially if it coincided with the need to refill the seed and superphosphate boxes on the Sunderseeder as they came around past the wagon where everything was stored. There'd be thick sandwiches and warm, sweet tea in improvised flasks - vinegar bottles wrapped round and round in layers of newspaper with thick, old socks pulled over all, were surprisingly effective. There were nose-bags for the horses and a brief time to lie in the sun for us, a time to dose and drowse in its warmth.

Once dinner and nose-bags were finished and team adjustments and replacements made, boxes were refilled and off they started on the long afternoon session of the day, and it was a long session as they worked until just before dark most days. For variety, or more truthfully, when Dad tired of our company and chatter on the job, we'd mess about on or near the wagon or go exploring nearby or just walk behind the dragging harrows round after round. The damp, crumbly soil was warm and caressing on our bare feet and the smell of freshly-turned earth something never to be had enough of. Oh, those sparkling, halcyon days when the sun shone after rain and we were charmed by the simplest pleasure. We envied no-one anything; in fact, we were sorry for anyone who wasn't us!

If he was working near the house, or on the home side of the main road, at the end of the day, Dad would uncouple the horses and let them make their own way home, just keeping two back to pull the wagon home. Then they'd plod down the road, one behind the other, heads down and tails swinging, weary after the long day's work. They were relieved of their collars and bridles at the harness shed and you could feel their relief as they bumped and rubbed their heads against their handlers, scratching itchy eyes bitten by flies during the day in spite of string flyveils and the castor oil Dad rubbed around their eyes as a preventative when flies were bad. They luxuriated as they rolled and wallowed in the loose, cool sand near the horse-yards, before making off to the dam for a drink. By now they were ravenous again and Dad used to say a horse would eat for twenty hours out of the twenty four if feed could be kept up to him.

Days began early when the team was working, as Dad would be up before dawn to give them their first feed. Often in those drowsy hours we stirred to hear the curiously hollow ring of his heavy boots as he clumped off, lantern in hand, to the horse-yards. Before they left for the day's work, nose-bags had to be made up with chaff, bran and oats and loaded into the wagon for the midday feed. The main tuck-in of the day was at knock-off time when sticky black molasses was added to the feed, then, last thing at night, the final one for the day. They were always looking out for him too, knickering in the dark as they saw the swinging lantern. All this time and effort and feeding when ten acres per day was considered pretty fair going with the Sunderseeder, by the time every animal was caught, bridled, groomed and collared and driven or led to the work site! In fact, sometimes it must have seemed that cropping was done solely to provide for the team, so it could work and provide for itself!

* * *

Chaff cutting, which was always done on Sunday mornings while we were all there to help, was one of the more irksome farm chores, though even that had its compensations if it meant a good rat hunt near the bottom of the stack. Everyone armed themselves with a makeshift cudgel and tied string bowyangs around their trouser legs as the rats were reputed to run up legs in their efforts to escape and no-one was taking any chances. As the bottom layers of the hay were disturbed, the rats appeared. Those that weren't flayed to death fell victims to the dogs - docile sheep dogs that became snarling, pouncing predators, diving between legs and flying sticks for a glorious burst of rare fun until all the rats were dispatched. But that was rare fun: most chaff cutting days were quite uneventful.

Mother would mix a bowl of treacle and sulphur powder and each of us had to swallow a large spoonful of this nauseating paste before we started as this was supposed to guard against the discomforts of chaff itch. Whether it actually did or not I don't know, but certainly none of us ever suffered unduly from the fine dust and flying fragments of hay that worked their way down the back of shirt necks and up sleeves and trouser legs. There was generally a bit of drama to look forward to when Dad started the reluctant old engine, and once there was more drama than expected when his hand slipped while making an adjustment and caught in the long drive belt from the engine to the chaff cutter. Before our astonished eyes, all six-foot three of him was picked up like a rag doll and slammed against the wall of the chaff house, making a dint in the iron and dislocating his shoulder. It was the end of chaff cutting for that day. None of us had ever seen Dad really hurt before and we were profoundly shaken. He never had to warn us again to keep clear of the drive belt.

Normally, after the engine was started, Dad fed the hay onto the cutter with Margaret cutting the twine on the sheaves before pushing it on to him. The rest of us kept up the supply to her from the stack. The cut chaff travelled up a kind of escalator to sift out into an ever-growing pile on the cool cement floor of the chaff house. It was boring, often hot, thirsty and thoroughly tiresome work, but it had to be done and by dint of goading, which Dad supplied with gusto whenever we looked like slowing down, we did it. There were no incentives either, like promised trips to swimming pools or frozen treats from a refrigerator to look forward to at the end of it - just a swig from a waterbag or a cup of tea, or maybe, if we were lucky, a watermelon cooling under a wet bag.

* * *

Drenching and shoeing were two jobs that had to be carried out regularly on the horses, hacks and team alike, while they were working - particularly shoeing, owing to the roughness of the country they worked on. Before Margaret and Bob became fully-fledged off-siders, Dad would have to enlist the aid of a neighbour in this day-long task. For we youngsters, watching with interest from a safe distance, both operations could be good spectator sports if one of the horses played up. But on the whole they became quite used to being shod and accepted it calmly and reasonably as a fact of life. It was laughable to see them all newly shod, stepping high in their new, heavy footwear until they became accustomed to the feel of it.

Drenching had its small excitements; a heavy winker bridle was put on the "patient" and, if all went well, it was led into the crush and a stout pole slipped fore and aft to prevent either backing out or lunging forward. A rope attached to the top of the bridle was slung up over the high cross bar of the crush and, when hauled on, dragged the animal's head up. A second operator, standing on something high, then prised the mouth open and emptied the medication into it from a bottle shoved far back in the mouth. There was a great deal of chomping and slobbering but most of it seemed to go down and have the desired effect.

* * *

There was another less dramatic way to get things moving, particularly if sand impaction was the trouble. Dad would rub the patient's withers vigorously with a smooth stone to irritate them. This led to a good hearty roll as a counter irritant, the theory being that the loosened sand would then be evacuated more easily and I suppose it worked.

* * *

There was one task popular with the whole family, mainly because it involved Mother coming out with us and that was a periodic day out poisongrubbing. Star thistles and York Road poison bush would have run riot on our hill slopes if neglected, so every now and again Dad would muster his work force and we'd make a day of it. On these sorties, Mother sat up on the wagon amongst a clutter of picks, mattocks, hoes, nose-bags, axes and fencing wire which was always taken "just in case", plus a wooden packing case holding our lunch and a blackened billy for tea-making.

Sometimes our search took us up onto the hills or down to Deadman's Valley. I don't know how this name came about but once Bob came home with an ancient and rusted bayonet he'd found down by the dam in Dead-man's. No-one could work out how it would have come to rest there, but there was a faintly mysterious air about that part of the farm. Big gums rustled darkly by the dam and there was a thicket of whispering casuarinas that it was always a relief to be clear of when mustering there. However, we three girls, drawing courage from numbers on more than one hot day, abandoned sheep and horses alike to their own devices for a brief plunge into the murky dam water before setting off on the long, dusty trek home.

* * *

There was one seasonal job that Dad would rarely let us accompany him on and that was harvesting. Bob and Margaret as they grew older, took over from the hired men we had from time to time and were generally the only ones to go out on the job, working to earn their passage. It was done, of necessity, in the heat of the day and there was no room on the machine for passengers and nothing much for "hangers on" to amuse themselves with while the team went round and round. As always there was an air of bustling urgency to get things started once conditions were right. The horses were all fat and fresh with big, broad, shiny rumps as they'd been "eating their heads off" since being turned out after seeding. Dust flew as they were yarded, caught and groomed and a good deal of that first morning was taken up with checking harness and gear to see that each animal was properly equipped before starting off for work.

They were nerve-wracking those first few round with the big, hulking harvester. Quail nested on the ground at this time of year, flying off their nests at the last minute when disturbed and with such a whirr of wings right under the horses' noses that it made them toss their heads and shy in their nervous collar-proud state. Everyone was on edge until a good healthy lather of sweat had broken out on the team and they'd felt their way back into their collars and once-familiar routine. After the first round, Dad checked the grain in the box to see that the machine was doing all that it should and producing a clean sample. He loved to chew the fresh wheat and tossed handfuls of it into his mouth at intervals during the day, coming home at night with the corners of his mouth all white from his day-long efforts. The kids relieved him on the machine once the horses had settled down and Bob took off his first entire harvest at the tender age of fourteen!

They were long, hot, dusty days - like the summers themselves; perhaps not in fact so different from now but there was so little relief from it then: no getting away or easy escape even to the beach though we were only a few miles from the coast. If we wanted to swim, most times we made do with a dip in the main dam not far from the house though, as the water level sank, this must have been a questionable practise as it was fouled daily by the cows that drank there. Gradually the creek dried, dry winds scorched in from the east, the land lay panting, waiting for the first sign of winter and the rains that would begin the whole cycle again.

CHAPTER 6

Our first school was at Waggrakine, a couple of miles from home and was opened in the early nineteen thirties. Ringed by gum trees, a new one of which was planted by the children each Arbor Day, it stood by the main road from Geraldton to Nanson, Nabawa and districts beyond. Little better than a shed, it was an "L"-shaped building of unlined, corrugated iron with a tiny back verandah and was elevated on short stumps. A rainwater tank at the back supplied our drinking requirements as well as catching the occasional rat.

One teacher, Miss Jean Webber, and after her, Mrs. Flo Speed, coped with all grades from "first bubs" to sixth standard. They must have done an incredible job ~ not only teaching us the three "R's" but having most of us in A grades by the time we went to town for schooling. All this was achieved by just plain chalk and talk - perseverance and pretty strenuous discipline, and not one of the teaching aids found in modern schools. To compound the difficulty, especially in the early days of Miss Webher's career, a great number of children could speak only limited, and in some cases, literally no English. A large percentage of bare, dusty feet and high garlic intake didn't do much to help, and on hot days when the walls fairly sizzled, conditions could be torrid, to say the least.

Many of us children walked to school - some of those sturdy little gardeners nearly four miles, morning and afternoon. Others rode bikes and some, horses. One day there was grief and consternation all round when an elderly horse lay down and died under the tree it was tied to, worn out from a life-time of servitude and tired to death of waiting.

Margaret and Bob used to ride old black Pride, then Jenny displaced Bob as pillion and he eventually came by an ancient bike which suited his mechanical instincts much better. When I started school, we girls all walked, though sometimes we were lucky enough to have a lift with a passerby, generally a gardener in a cart. Motor cars seldom went by and we usually had the road to ourselves.

Memories of the little school are vague and jumbled now, as it was half way through my first year that the bus started running us in to the school in Geraldton. But I do remember that the Macedonian kids introduced a strange game called "pig". From memory, more brawn than brain was necessary to score and, being the youngest, I only made up numbers when no-one else would play. There was, too, a dam in a nearby paddock that was supposed to be strictly out of bounds to all pupils. However, on hot days, the bigger boys would melt mysteriously away from the schoolyard and then muffled whoops and shouts would float across to us who were left behind. Poor teacher could only confront the culprits after the event and they were fortunate there were never any mishaps, as I doubt that many of us could swim to save ourselves or anyone else.

And who could forget the adroitness of the brothers Steve and Jim in disposing of any fly unwise enough to settle even lightly on either of their faces in school. Without any animation or change of expression whatsoever, either one could bring up his right hand in a lightning-quick gesture, trapping the intruder with two fingers. By the end of the day there was always a neat little pile of dead flies on each of their desks.

Then there was a school excursion up onto one of the hills and into the caves and a picnic in a creek bed with shady gums and a lone quandong tree and a myriad bull ants struggling to an ecstatic if watery death in a tub of lukewarm raspberry vinegar. Oh yes - and getting the "cuts" along with the other kids for being late to school after dawdling to pick and suck the end of a red creeper than grew flat on the ground and yielded a speck of nectar for our troubles. And on hot, hot afternoon walks home, gouging up the bubbles of melting tar that blistered in the heat on the main road and sticking pebbles onto the heels of our shoes to give a mincing, high-heeled effect. And Dad coming out to meet us one afternoon in a storm, bringing wheat bags to help keep off a little of the wet; and Mother having hot cocoa and fresh damper ready for us in the kitchen.

The older boys must have been a fairly rebellious lot as even in my short school career there I can remember one of them firing a whole nest full of rotten eggs, brought to school for the specific purpose, defiantly around the yard. Someone else put a bob-tailed goanna in teacher's drawer with most satisfactory results for the expectant class and, as a final rebellious gesture, the cane was spirited away and found sometime later, broken into small pieces and stuffed down a rabbit burrow.

At the break-up concert before the school closed, every child contributed a poem or song and there were costumes for every part in the little plays. We were quiet and thoughtful as we clip-clopped home in the landau behind Prince that night, watching his shod hooves strike tiny sparks on the road metal, happy with our efforts but vaguely apprehensive about the new venture ahead, for it was nineteen thirty-nine and the school bus was to begin taking us into town. The little school has long since disappeared. It stood for some time, snug amongst the trees by the road until it was removed, holus-bolus, to do further service as a farm shed. Now, only the trees remain.

* * *

In modern jargon, I think the term "traumatic experience" would have described my transition from a one-teacher bush school to one accommodating the many and varied needs of several hundred town children. Perhaps it was harder for me being very young, anyway, traumatic or not, the change was inevitable and off I rattled with the others on the box-like grey bus (a Chev Maple Leaf, I'm told) to school in town. Not having had a motor vehicle in the family in my lifetime, this in itself was a new and fairly bewildering experience at first but with the rest of them I managed to cultivate a few of the tactics necessary for survival on a bus, spartan to say the least in its appointments and crowded with a fairly unruly lot of kids.

Part of our daily journey was along the Bluff Point Road and as we trundled back and forth, often the rank pong of seaweed was strong in the air. Some enmity grew between the State School kids and those who attended the Convent and Christian Brothers College, but this mostly took the form of name calling and the recital of such choice ditties as: "Convent dogs, sitting on logs - Eating maggots out of frogs" to which they would reply in like kind. It was one way of filling in the time on a long, wearisome journey, and for some it was a long journey. Apart from nodding off to sleep, there was one other way, and that was to sing; some of the bigger girls sang quite well and we'd all join in where we could - cowboy songs mostly. Over the years, I think "Red River Valley" was the most sung and though I've heard it rendered in many different places and in different languages too, it is still, to me, the most nostalgic of songs; a kind of school bus anthem.

In spite of its constant use and long daily journeys, the old bus rarely broke down or gave any trouble that we knew of. It wasn't fast, in fact if we felt we were going faster then usual, we'd peep over Mr. Carr's shoulder to read the speedo and it was rarely above thirty miles per hour. But that was enough to make the canvas blinds at the windows flap in a hectic tattoo where the buttons were missing and the whole bus shudder so that we had to hang onto the narrow wooden plank-like seats around the sides and back, or the one down the middle where the smaller children sat, or rather perched. There was only one "near miss" incident involving the bus but that comes later.

I believe I was in "second bubs" on moving in to the town school and my first teacher was a young lady I remember for the smoothness and shininess of her shoulder-length black hair. The most appalling thing that happened to me in those first few days was that I repeatedly had to stand up and tell her my Christian name and how to pronounce and spell it as committing this information to memory seemed to be quite beyond her. For a bush child among strangers, believe me this was appalling, and night after night, I'd go to sleep wishing with all my heart that by some miracle I'd wake up in the morning to find that my name was Pat or Mary or anything that people could say and spell without any help from me. Grandpa was the one I had to thank for my plight. Enga was a native name, he said, from the tribe that lived around the area where he was a boy, and when I was born, Mother had given in to the old man's wishes, putting aside Deborah, which she favoured.

Our classroom was crowded and smelt of chalk and warm bodies and little school cases with their conglomerate contents and I remember feeling acutely lonely at being separated from the older three kids in the family, as previously, though in different classes, they'd always at least been in the same room. Now we'd all been "drafted" like sheep into separate classrooms and I was surrounded by small strangers. At least there was some compensation to be had from being up to date with our work and one of the earliest reading books I recall, told of the domestic escapades of a pair of rabbit youngsters, Billy and Betty, who with their parents had a neat underground hideout and spent a good deal of time getting out of scrapes with predatory human beings. In the pictures, Billy wore knicker-bockers and Betty a tiny skirt that stuck out to reveal singularly muscular and athletic-looking thighs - even for a rabbit who spent most of her time on the run!

Later came the red Oxford reading books with tales of "Brenda the Cowgirl ", "Daisy and the Apples", "The Poppy-seed Lady" and "The Brave Girl" who waved her scarlet, flannel petticoat in time to stop a train that would otherwise have crashed into a washed-out railway bridge. Then there was another story that upset me greatly after I found out what the word "devoured" meant. It was about a little goat who went up on the mountain every day with the herd but decided not to come down one evening when the herd boy called them. I guess he just wanted to "do his own thing" for once, but stories then didn't allow for such rebelliousness and there were no second chances for children and little goats who didn't do as they were told. So after some heart-stopping drama, the wolf devoured him and his little adventure was over. I could hardly bear to pick up the book after that in case it opened to show the little creature, terrified and alone, being stalked by the villainous-looking wolf, his tongue lolling in anticipation.

In time we learned to spell lists of words from Schonell Spellers and recited tables by the hour: and in higher classes, sang an odd and somehow irrelevant song called "Where the Bee Sucks, There Suck I". Lord, where did they get them from! For me, reading, writing and spelling were all plain sailing and ballad-type poetry a joy. History at primary level was only moderately interesting, while geography was decidedly more so as it was about those faraway places that were to beckon so irresistibly later and the people who lived in those places.

There was a vast assembly hall in the school with a stage at one end and classrooms leading off it. Every Friday morning we'd have to assemble before going to our classes and, amongst other things, sing "God Save the King" and other legendary and patriotic songs like "Land of Hope and Glory", "There'll Always be an England" and "The British Grenadiers", though for years I laboured under the misapprehension that it was "The British Grand Ideas"! My tentative squeak was entirely lost in that throaty throng anyway, so I went happily on, thinking it rather a strange song and trying to fit the words to the tune at the fade-out point and never quite making it.

The playground at the Geraldton Primary School then was largely a barren waste with several squawking iron swings surrounded by a stand of castor oil bushes, a few gum trees around one side of the perimeter and what must have been a couple of acres of potholed playing area. I believe there was a cricket pitch over near the "manual" shed and a long row of seating down one side of the classrooms. One section of playground that was out-of-bounds to little ones, led past the toilets and more castor oil bushes to a mysterious place referred to by the bigger kids as something that sounded like "Dommy Sigh". Actually it was the Domestic Science Block, used only by seniors and High School girls. A poor exasperated Miss Partridge was to labour with me when my turn came, in the art of making jam roly-poly, removing tea stains from starched white table cloths and making strange and unwearable articles on a foot-operated sewing machine.

Back in the playground there were two sheds, one each for boys and girls, where we had to eat our lunch. A tap outside each offered, as far as I can remember, the only drinking facilities we had. If there was a rush on, we just had to wait our turn. Those lunches were the plague of Mother's life. Sometimes she had as many as seven to cut before the bus came in the morning: five for us school children and one each for Dad and his off-sider if he was doing seasonal working and staying out all day. There were no short cuts either; every slice had to be cut by hand and there was never anything exciting to put in sandwiches. How she must have enjoyed weekends when at least, even though work had to go on, there were no cries of, "Here comes the bus! The bus is coming!"

Pupils of the original Waggrakine School with teacher, Jean Webber (later Mrs Trant) before the bus run took us to school in Geraldton.

* * *

There's a paddock not far from where our little bush school used to be, that was owned by the Anglican Church and for many years Dad had the lease on it. There was, and still is, a small, stone cottage there under the hills about eight miles from Geraldton. When the cottage was built in the early eighteen seventies by the Reverend C.G. Nicolay, the small steep roof was thatched, but the roofing was later replaced with red corrugated iron. The Reverend Nicolay was appointed Chaplain at Geraldton in eighteen seventy, arriving in Fremantle on the "Lady Louisa" on April the twenty-fifth of that year, and, soon after moving to Geraldton, in June, he recommended that an experimental coffee plantation be established in the area. The climate seemed similar to that of some parts of Brazil, where coffee flourished, and where he had served as chaplain to British residents of Bahia for some years previously.

Governor Weld authorised the Valley of Waggrakine to be set aside as a reserve for coffee cultivation and the Reverend Nicolay took on the task of development. His' son joined him in this venture and coffee seed from Aden and later Brazil was planted. However, after three years, the failure of the project was all too evident and sale of the reserve was recommended. For many years the little holding was satirically known by Geraldton townfolk as "The Coffee Plantation". A wide scarp which runs around the hill behind the cottage was made about nineteen ten, being intended as part of a water supply for Geraldton. A catchment area was prepared at the back of the hill, but like the coffee plantation before it, it was unsuccessful, and never put to use.

Just by the house is the original stone-lined well and, according to our legend at least, it was haunted - by the ghost of an old man who drowned there long ago. No-one knew quite what old man, but on certain nights his ghost, wearing a night shirt and ringing a bell, was reputed to rise from the depths of the well. Margaret and Bob and some of their pals used to set rabbit traps in the valley beyond the house, making a final round of inspection in the early evening and generally arriving home just after dark. The history of the old house was mentioned from time to time and along with it, a comment on the likelihood or otherwise of the ghost. The brave trappers scoffed at the notion, but being kids, and pretty adventurous ones at that, some curiosity was aroused that wouldn't be satisfied by anything less than eye witness.

So, one evening, when the moon was reckoned to be in the right quarter, they decided the time had come to wait and watch and either see or dismiss for themselves this nocturnal phenomenon. They took up their positions in a shallow gutter, a safe distance from the house but close enough to have a good view, "just in case". The boys' bikes were propped nearby and Margaret's horse hitched to the nearest tree. The lantern, though left alight, was hidden from view. Silence fell on the little group as the moon rose, full and silver, and doubt and apprehension gripped each thudding heart and squeezed with steely fingers. Then "something" got out of the well! No-one waited to see what! They moved as one in a frantic getaway, on desperately wobbling bikes and startled horse, progress impeded by limp, dangling rabbits and clattering traps and lamp. Francis and Graham took off in the direction of their homes down the road and Bob and Margaret to theirs.

Mother was worried when they weren't home by their usual time and went to the sleepout door several times to look up the road for them. Time ticked on, then, on the still night air came the sound of hooves drumming down the road, at first like a fluttering heartbeat, but growing louder every second. Within minutes Margaret, white-faced and breathless, flung into the dining room where we were all sitting, followed in an incredibly short time by Bob, eyes big as saucers and cheeks bright from furious pedalling. Fear had put wings on his decrepit bike as nothing else could! The pong that floated from the fizzing, spluttering carbide lamp he still clutched in his hand was heavy on the air.

The silence that followed such a dramatic entry was brief and intense.

Both kids were too out of breath to offer any explanation, so Dad took the situation firmly in hand. Pointing at the lamp, he bellowed at Bob, "Get that stinking thing out of here!" Poor Bob was soon brought down to reality, and clumped outside with the offending lamp. Explanations seemed pointless after that. The spell was lost, and no-one would believe anyway. Grandpa, knowing by instinct what they had been up to, muttered, "Silly kids! Silly kids! Frightening themselves like that!" Perhaps it had all been imagination, but from then on, any trapping done in the valley near the old house was finished well before dark. Mother always maintained that any self-respecting ghost would steer well clear of that smelly lamp, anyway, but they took no more chances.

For some time after that, an elderly couple occupied the house. The old man did some work for Dad and sometimes his wife came over to visit Mother, driving a little sulky. She'd hitch the horse to a big wattle tree near the wire fence on the way to the dub - a tree that many years before had been split open by lightning. Mother said the old lady was a gypsy, and certainly there was something exotic about her, with her bright, dark eyes and swarthy complexion, the illusion sometimes enhanced by the coloured scarf she wore over her head. Gypsy or not, she could talk, and even as a small child I was impressed by her garrulousness - about how we children had grown since her last visit, who we were like, how she had never had children of her own, about Harry her big tabby cat, about anything, and it was all delivered in a high-pitched nasal tone with a Cockney accent to boot.

It was she who taught Jenny to knit, Jenny in turn teaching me, using nails and bits of string. But more than her knitting or her talking, what impressed us most about the lady was her marvellous upper denture! The teeth were set in what appeared to be rubber, that's what it looked like, anyway, and not only rubber, but bright orange at that. This denture was highly mobile and while its owner was engaged in conversation, seemed to take on a life of its own, slipping and cavorting at will, and making no pretence at following the formation of the spoken word. But she was nothing daunted and kept cheerfully on, regardless, and oblivious to our fascinated stares.

After they moved out to live in town, the little house was empty again. There were, and still are, I hope, two fig trees growing close by and whenever we mustered sheep in the paddock, we'd ride over to eat as many of the ripe figs as we could. With their smooth, bright green skins and squashy, red flesh, they were different from our Adam and turkey figs at home and, accordingly, had a flavour of their own.

During the war when troops were camped all over the area, the little house was used as Officers' Headquarters, coming alive with a glorious burst of activity and importance that seemed to justify its very existence. For a while its heart beat with life and the sounds of living: the shrill of a field telephone, voices giving orders, taking orders, the clump of heavy boots. And the hills echoed back the sound of army trucks and a despatch rider's motorbike.

Now, uninhabited since those years except by sheep in search of shade or night shelter, it is in great disrepair, part of the roof being off and general signs of neglect and misuse all too evident. Rust-coloured tears seem to ooze from the empty window frames and stain the stone walls below. Still it stands, aloof and just a little reproachful, dignified and just a little mysterious, a scrap of history all but forgotten, silently weeping in the shadow of the timeless hills.

CHAPTER 7

When war broke out in Europe, naturally the word had little meaning for us, except that we knew things were going on and somehow it was just a little exciting. The tall, stern-faced, black radio in the dining room gave out with static-ridden speeches and we were continually being shushed or sent outside so Dad could listen to the news. Only in his more reflective moods had he told us about that other terrible war; of the mud and filth and lice of the trenches and of the misty, chilling rain that seemed perpetually to shroud the grey countryside of France. He told us about the big horsedrawn guns - the eighteen pounders, he called them - and of the soul-tearing sight and sound of wounded and dying horses when occasionally a shell landed behind the lines and exploded amongst them where they were tied up; and of a game little black saddle mare he called Kitty. We heard about the cook, universally and without malice known as Sango the Bastard. Then there was the tough, wry-humoured little soldier who handled the great black South American mules in the lumbering General Service wagons, bawling at them in their cussedness, "Come on you long-eared Jerusalem so-and-so's!" And the fresh-faced American soldiers, "beardless boys" he called them, who joined them in the trenches and died in their thousands, believing it was a skirmish that would all be over in few weeks and that they'd soon be back in their beloved America.

There was another impression that was to stay with him till the end of his days - an unstinted admiration for Tommy Atkins, the ordinary, average British soldier who, so many times, he saw ride straight to almost certain death with scarcely a backward glance. Then there was a time when they were guarding a group of German prisoners, young men like themselves, covered with the same mud and lice and a feeling of helpless futility and muteness in the air; no-one able to communicate with the other, no way of saying, "Well, how are things with you, Fritz?" Nothing but a sullen, abysmal silence and hostile stares: nothing for either side to do but huddle away from the mizzling rain and wish to God for the whole damn thing to be over. There was a military hospital, too, and death and delirium all round and ever-present as Spanish Flu spread its grim mantle.

Mother had her memories, too, all sad and rarely spoken of. There had been a beloved eider brother, just twenty, shot down on Gallipoli, and the farewells at railway stations as endless, grey troop trains pulled out, packed with eager young men going to the war, while the band played, "There's a Long, Long, Trail A-Winding". There were the deaths of almost all the friends of her brothers, often themselves looked on as brothers. They were memories better left undisturbed.

For us, however, nothing seemed much different at first. We'd started going to school in town towards the end of that year and that made the biggest change in our lives. As time went on, we heard mention of some commodities that were scarce or unprocurable. Rubber was one of these and when erasing mistakes in our homework, we found that a piece of soft bread balled up was quite effective for pencil at least. Rice puddings were a thing of the past, so Mother decided we should try boiled wheat. After all, there were stories of how people existed on boiled wheat during the Depression, and we had plenty on hand.

Dad produced a clean sample of grain and Mother boiled it after soaking it for

Margaret, Bob, Enga, David and Jenny with Grandpa.

a while. She tried it and said it needed more cooking; and then some. At last it was pronounced ready and we began in high anticipation. Well, we chewed and chewed and chewed some more - all in stony silence. It was the greatest meal time conversation stopper a head of the house could have wished for! Our jaws ached and face muscles felt as though they bulged from the effort. After several attempts along the same lines, I think we just resigned ourselves to the unavailability of rice and left it at that.

Petrol became scarce, not that this concerned us much as we had no vehicle anyway, but private transport and the school bus went about powered by smelly gas producers, and the only kind of tea cups to be had were of glass, generally tinted pale green, from memory. You had to remember to stand a teaspoon in them before pouring anything in as this was supposed to absorb the heat and save the cup from cracking. Ration books were introduced for clothing and some grocery lines, and at school, trenches were dug around the edge of the playground. We had regular air-raid drill now, and the town seemed full of men in uniform.

One day our Uncle Ellison, Mother's youngest brother, came to school to say goodbye to us before he went to the war. It was in the afternoon, just as we were boarding the bus to come home and I remember being almost overwhelmed by the solemnity of the occasion and shy pride to think that all the kids watching knew this tall, fair-haired young man, looking so splendid in his uniform, was our uncle. He didn't say much, just hugged us all in turn and his uniform felt rough and scratchy against my cheek and smelt of newness and tobacco. I remember too feeling slightly puzzled and just a little disappointed that he walked away then without looking back and didn't stay to wave us off as I'd hoped he would.

Granny came out from town to live with us then and shared the long sleepout with us five children. Grandpa kept his tiny bedroom at the end of the kitchen, where sunflowers nodded at the window and a razor strop hung behind the door and there was just room enough for all of us around the main kitchen table. Occasionally Granny would treat us to some of her fabulous puff or flaky pastries, as she loved to cook and seemed to make treats out of the most spartan ingredients. Granny had a soft spot for Jenny as a little girl, and taught her to sew on an ancient hand-operated Singer machine, while it seemed a tacit agreement that I, who was three years younger, was Grandpa's "pet", a word I detested.

Everyday we'd go with him to collect the eggs and feed the chooks, with me staying as close as possible to him, as I loathed the flying feathers and clucking that went with fowls. The backs of Grandpa's sunburnt hands often bore scratches, a legacy from his encounters with a particularly aggressive rooster or broody hens that had to be foisted off nests and carried, head down and squawking, to the little pen where they were left to "cool off" for a few days. Jenny was much braver than I; brave enough to carry the hens like Grandpa, pink in the face and very determined, while he kept the rooster at bay with his walking stick. The idea filled me with real horror.

At the time, we were only young children and didn't notice, but in later life, when I stopped to think about it, it seemed strange that after all their years of association through close family connections and more years of living under the one roof, Grandpa and Granny remained to each other Mr. Mills and Mrs. Mountain. It was almost as though they were still waiting to be properly introduced. Never, never did either refer to the other by Christian name in direct conversation or through a third party.

After a while the army took over several areas of our farm and quite sophisticated little tent settlements flourished amongst the hills. The men were waiting to be sent overseas, to the New Guinea area, I believe. Up till then we'd been free to roam at will on our horses, but now there were certain areas out-of-bounds and strictly forbidden to us, and we had instructions from our parents never to dismount while there were soldiers around and to stay together at all times. On the whole, the troops were quite well-behaved, though there were some incidents - either deliberate or just plain thoughtless - like taking a bath, soap and all, in a sheep trough, or busting fences in Bren Gun carriers and busting through in a new place on the return journey: rickety fences some of them, but all important nevertheless. And one hot, gusty afternoon there was a spectacular fire started by a carelessly discarded cigarette butt.

Dad was flattered when some of the soldiers took pictures of the team, telling him it was the finest lot of horses they'd seen since leaving their home states. But one day he came home in high dudgeon. Later it transpired that on the way home that evening a truck full of soldiers had gone by and one youngster had leaned over and called out what was probably meant to be a perfectly innocent and cheerful greeting, "Hi, Pop!" Dad was outraged. He would have been just about fifty then and a fine, straight figure of a man, and nobody had ever called him Pop before. "Bloody bit of a kid. I'll give him Pop!"

Shearers were at a premium now as all the young men in the district had joined up or were at home caring for their own places. One season with fly strike amongst the sheep and desperate to get the shearing through, Dad approached the Commanding Officer of the camp to see if there were a couple of men who could come and do the job. It was arranged at last and they turned up, keen to be back in familiar harness and glad of the diversion from army life. Colin was a quiet young man from New South Wales who told us that at home, as well as being a shearer, he kept bees. This seemed to Jenny and I an extremely hazardous and eccentric thing to do, and for the duration of his stay he was regarded with a mixture of respect and puzzlement.

Jack was an immediate favourite with us all. A tall, lanky young soldier from Rockhampton, he cracked jokes with us and whistled through his teeth as he rolled his smokes. The very fact of his coming from faraway Queensland - Granny's country - enhanced him in our eyes, but most of all we liked him for his unfailing good humour that seemed to embrace all things and conditions. I can never to this day hear the song "You Are My Sunshine" without remembering Jack. He sang it all day, every day at work and after work when they played cricket with us on the flat near the house, using the stump of a cockatoo bush for a wicket and a roughly hewn board for a bat. Sometimes he sang it with a gay flourish, other times with a truly plaintive throb. Every unresponsive old ewe and struggling wether that crossed the board was serenaded: "You are my Sunshine, my only Sunshine . . ." We kids had lumps in our throats the day Jack rolled his swag and went back to camp. We lost track of him after he was sent overseas, but I'd like to think that when it was all over, he went home to Queensland to find his Sunshine.

All this time the possibility of a Japanese invasion grew more real and many families left the town, evacuating often to more remote inland places. Plans were made for our flight too, and Dad went about looking preoccupied and adding to and crossing off a list of stock and stores to be taken when the time came. Although the subject was never openly discussed, we heard enough bits and pieces of conversation amongst the adults to fill in the rest for ourselves. Four of the soundest and most reliable team horses were to be taken for the wagon, plus a saddle horse and Wendy, the stout-hearted, irascible Timor pony we'd learned to ride on, and which had dumped us all in turn, without ceremony. Drinking water, stores and all essential gear were to be stowed on the wagon, along with some fodder for the horses. The rest they would have to forage for as they went along. This wouldn't have left much room for passengers - six of them, discounting the two out-riders and Grandpa, who firmly elected to stay behind - so I guess some footslogging was planned which would have slowed things down considerably. What a pathetic little convoy we would have made, especially to an airborne enemy! But we kids who had pored over the adventures of "poor" people and

Enga with Grandpa in the buggy.

some of Ion Idriess's sagas of the outback, were fired with anticipation. This was real adventure! The only thing that concerned us was what would happen to Grandpa and the animals that were left behind. Dad told us later that he would have opened the gates and let the stock loose to fend for themselves and presumably run from the Japs too. As for Grandpa, who knows. He was quite adamant that he wasn't coming, anyway; he was an old man and ready to take his chance.

Days turned into weeks. The list was taken out and pondered over and put away. News broadcasts were listened to as though our lives depended on it, as well they could have. Then, the crisis passed. The list was torn up and there was to be no adventure, just school and the daily round as usual. I do remember being bitterly disappointed, though, with hindsight can only imagine the relief Dad and Mother must have felt at not having to organise such an expedition.

At least one thing happened about this time to enliven our daily routine, even if it wasn't as disruptive as evacuation. There was a particularly chilly winter night when unusually heavy fog blanketed the valley and surrounding hills. The dogs were restless during the early hours of next morning and Dad got up several times to investigate the cause, but at first could see nothing unusual apart from the fog. When they persisted in their barking in spite of his hearty admonitions to lie down, he saw, down by the dam, the light from a couple of lanterns, flickering dully as they were swung about, and heard excited voices; unusual, but perhaps a cow had got into one of the gardens and was being hunted out. Grandpa called out from his room, wanting to know what the racket had been up on the hill, but Dad, having heard nothing himself, dismissed that query as curtly as he did the dogs, and went back to bed.

Next morning, as he was stoking the fire to boil the first kettle of the day, the dogs began barking again, furiously this time, and wouldn't be quietened as they rushed out across the ram paddock. Dad started after them this time, but didn't get far. There, making his way out of the fog, was the forlorn and damp figure of a young man in R.A.A.F. uniform! The dogs were mad with excitement now, and Dad roared at them again as he escorted our uninvited guest to the warmth of the kitchen, leaving all questions to later. It turned out that he'd been heading for the airfield several miles further on, but by misadventure in the bad conditions, had perched his craft, a twin-engined Avro Anson, on the edge of a hill less than a mile from the house.

He'd sat tight in what was left of it till morning light, then, stepping out of the cockpit, had sustained the only injuries of the whole episode, grazes and scratches, when he slithered down the almost sheer face of that part of the hill! The fog was still dense and he couldn't see the house, but took his bearings from the dogs' barking and Dad's voice, stumbling down the remainder of the hill and bumping into fences and startled rams before arriving. He was withdrawn and disconsolate as Mother gave him hot tea in front of the stove and cleaned up his superficial wounds. It was a miracle he'd survived at all, but he gave the distinct impression that he'd have preferred to make a good job of it rather than go back and face the authorities.

It wasn't long before several of the gardeners arrived, wanting to know if we'd heard anything during the night, and they were full of animated exclamations and sympathetic noises when they heard the news. For a while the old kitchen almost bulged at the seams as they milled about, jabbering and gesticulating, and we kids with eyes as big as saucers thought all our Christmases had come at once as far as things happening were concerned. The poor young man, certainly in a state of shock, probably wished he'd stayed perched on the hill at that stage. But routine took over; there were cows to be milked, school lunches to cut and a bus to be caught, so we reluctantly went our various ways. One of the gardeners took the airman into town in his truck and for a couple of days, Air Force personnel came backwards and forwards to survey the scene and pick up the wreckage that was strewn about and dangling on trees over the whole area.

It was not long after this that Grandpa died. His last few weeks were spent entirely between his little room and the side verandah where he sat in his cane chair in the sun, wearing a heavy black overcoat against the danger of chills and a pith helmet that seldom left his head, probably for the same reason. He seldom read and spoke less, just sat there day after day, keeping warm and thinking of the Lord knows what that happened so long ago. Mother said he lived in the past and there was a lot of past to reflect on as he was nearly eighty-four by then. With his coppery, sun-burnished skin and high cheekbones, I thought secretly that he looked like an old Indian holding court, and living in the past or not, he knew everything that was going on, and I believed him when once he said he "had eyes in the back of his head."

Bishop Frewer, the Anglican Bishop of the Northwest, and, the Anglican Minister from town, came to visit and the old man took communion as he'd done on previous occasions when the Bishop called. I remember Bishop Frewer as a small, neat man, straight-backed and rosy-cheeked despite his years of exposure to the harsh Northwest sun. He wore a purple waistcoat and whenever he came to afternoon tea, sat up very straight on the edge of his chair and spoke in a soft quick manner.

Mother did what she could for Grandpa when he became ill and coughed so distressingly, but when he couldn't move from his bed, it became too much for her and he went to hospital in town where he died peacefully a few days later; a grand old bushman and almost our last link with the "old" days. We knew he wasn't coming back because his knobbly-headed, bush-cut walking stick was left behind, propped in a corner of the room where it was to stay for many years to come. There was such a humble handful of possessions left after such a long life; just a few clothes and pith helmet, a couple of books, a pair of tiny, round spectacles in a little case that looked as though it had been made from some kind of soft bark, and a square box that sat on his chest of drawers and was furnished with panels of porcupine quills. It held a few personal treasures like tiny, faded photographs and letters, and that was about all. Eventually Granny moved into the little room and once again we spaced out the iron bedsteads in the long sleepout.

CHAPTER 8

With all our hectic childhood activity and work about the farm, it was a wonder none of us hurt ourselves seriously. There were so many scrapes and scraps and odd incidents - like having one's toes trodden heavily upon and leaned on a little by one of the cows at milking time. Believe me, there is nothing more unmovable than a contented cow as she forages about good humouredly amongst the contents of her feed bin, likely as not flipping you in the eye with the tip of her tail as she does so, oblivious to the accompanying shouts of rage and hammering of small fists on her flank. Eventually she may deign to turn and regard this display of frenzied activity with her large bovine eyes moist and sympathetic and bits of chaff dangling foolishly from her muzzle and whiskers, without doing a thing to remedy the situation, until one's poor appendage is almost crushed into the ground! As for falls from horses, we had so many between us that we simply lost count.

Generally the worst that happened was a well-shaken pride and a few bruises that faded anyway, until the next time. There was one rotund old bay mare that Jenny and I came off quite regularly when double dinking bareback. Her back was so broad and shiny that there was nothing to save us once we had a lean on. We'd come down in a giggling, squealing heap and old Wassy would hardly cock an ear in our direction as she munched on the nearest clump of grass, waiting for us to sort ourselves out and climb on board again.

Not all of our hacks were so accommodating though, and there was one she-devil of a white mare called Dolly who was so tall and graceful it was hard to imagine her as being anything but angelic by nature. One of the young shearers who came to our place regularly then, took a fancy to Dolly. He could ride a bit and wasn't going to be satisfied until he'd tried her out. So, one evening after work, Lionel announced that he'd take Dolly, who was tied up next to the shearing shed, and ride up to the box for the mail. By this time we were getting all our bread from town on the twice-weekly mail truck and Lionel was warned that there would be several loaves to pick up, but he was quite sure that he and Dolly would manage. So, taken in by her pristine, milk-white beauty, he mounted and started off up the Mail Gate road.

In fairness to Dolly, she had done a day's work and like any self-respecting horse, was thoroughly soured by the idea of heading away from home and not towards the horseyards at that time of day. So she reefed and jogged and crab-walked and did everything possible to register her protest at this turn of events. However, at last they arrived at the mail box. There wasn't much mail, but as expected, there were five loaves, large as life, and wrapped in thin paper. Lionel put the mail down the front of his shirt and managed to fit one of the loaves there too. The other four had to be carried, two under each arm, probably to the horse, giving him a strange winged appearance as he approached to remount for the trip home. The mare snorted in alarm and cautiously backed off but Lionel managed to calm her down with pats and gentle words until he felt she was reassured. He was right as he put his foot in the stirrup but with the effort of swinging his right leg over her back, the paper rustled ominously and this was just too much for Dolly. As she plunged forward, Lionel hit the saddle with a wallop, groping

The author on Wassy — aged about 10.

wildly for his right stirrup and hanging on for dear life to both horse and bread as she careered off down the road to home, bolting in a blind panic. There was no hope of pulling her up, it was just a case of hanging on and staying with her in her crazy haste to be home.

We heard them coming down the road and they went past the house like a whirlwind - the lovely white mare with her nostrils flaring crimson and her white mane and tail streaming like a mythical horse, while poor Lionel clung to the reins and saddle for dear life, still with only one foot in the stirrup and his shirt front distended grotesquely with the one remaining loaf of bread. Down through the trees they dodged, scaring the daylights out of the busy, foraging hens in their way and making all the dogs bark until at the horseyard at last, Dolly pulled up in a tremendous cloud of dust, almost shooting her unfortunate rider right over her ears, but, game to the last, he managed to hang on. It was a very subdued horseman who dismounted that evening, vowing never to get on a horse again and most certainly never a white one! Dad walked back up the road to find the other loaves of bread that had been scattered like substantial chunks of manna from Heaven at intervals, and dust them off. They laughed about it over tea that night when Lionel had related the whole episode in detail for the umpteenth time but he knew he'd been lucky to get out of it with nothing more than a bad fright.

Apart from her tendency to bolt, Dolly was a dead loss as a hack. She never wanted to leave home and once she was persuaded to go, was rough and uneven in her gait. So she was put into the buggy shafts where, surprisingly, she behaved herself quite well. However, we had several horses that could be used in the buggy, so eventually she was sold to an elderly couple who lived near Bluff

Enga on Thunder, Margaret on Joe — a later, more stylish acquisition.

Point, just out of Geraldton. They had her for years after that and often as we went past on the school bus we'd see the three of them getting along at their own pace and letting the rest of the world go by - the white mare in her little winker bridle and the old pair sitting close together in the sulky, all suiting each other down to the ground.

And if Dolly was worth a mention, the story wouldn't be complete without a small segment at least on Thunder. What a character! Quite a handsome old grey he was and the cunningest nag God ever stuck legs on: not mean or vicious, just plain cunning.

Thunder hated to be caught in the first place, presenting his rump to anyone approaching with a bridle and swinging his head from side to side while describing a small semi-circles until his would be catcher was livid with frustration, where-upon he'd sail off with head and tail up, looking quite splendid in his victory. So Dad hobbled him. Thunder took up the challenge like a true champion and became airborne - sailing over five wire fences, hobbles and all.

When eventually he was cornered, saddled and mounted, he gave one the roughest ride imaginable. He wasn't a good walker or trotter and seemed deliberately to get off on the wrong foot when cantering so that one was jarred to the core and had to pull up and start again while he sorted his legs out. Dad took him out once to do some sheep work and led him most of the way home rather than ride "the rough old so and so. Shake a man's teeth out!" So Thunder ended up winning anyway.

But there was something that could ensnare and turn him into a drooling, slobbering old softie, catchable anywhere, anytime and that something was figs. No need to hobble Thunder in the fig season. Once he caught a whiff of the proffered fruit, he was helpless to resist and would come up with neck out-stretched and lips mumbling and submit to being caught. In fact, our cousin Rachel Percy who spent holidays with us from time to time and still remembers Thunder with bemused affection, wrote a piece for the Womens' Session called "*A Fig For Thunder*," which summed him up entirely.

Getting back to my original statement of none of us ever having a serious injury, it really was a wonder as we always had bits of skin off somewhere and had never heard of tetanus immunisation, so were just plain lucky, I guess, with regard to that. Bob had a couple of spectacular falls into the sheep dip at different times - plunging vigorously with his forked pole at the sheep's necks as they swam past to submerge them but missing and in his effort, overbalancing himself on top of the startled animals. Fortunately he didn't swallow any of the arsenically-based compound or he could have been a very sick boy. Another time he was helping Dad spread superphosphate with the funnel-like broadcaster on the back of the wagon and Kate and Blossom getting along at a good smart trot. Dad was driving this day and Bob, thinking no doubt to save time and be helpful, stood up to refill the broadcaster, while still in motion. The super was heavy and just as the kid got his arms around the half empty bag and had it poised, the wagon hit a substantial bump. For a split second he was airborne, embracing what looked like a stout and lifeless partner in a strange fandango! Super dust shot into his face as the bag came down hard on the ground, half blinding him, while the wagon went on its merry way, Dad all unaware of his offsider's untimely defection.

As far as sickness went, I can't remember anything worse than the usual childish ailments, though at one time Mother said she had all the eldest three down with whooping cough and Margaret a very sick little girl indeed. Coughs and colds were treated with Heenzo, a cough mixture which she made up with large quantities from a bottle of concentrate, and Vick's Vaporub applied vigorously to chests and backs. And how we squirmed and grizzled and tried to wriggle away because her hands were rough from hard work and doing everything the hard way. Occasionally we'd all be treated with a dose of oil from the slender blue bottle on the kitchen dresser and now and then we'd have a bottle of codliver oil and malt to get through.

One thing that did plague us from time to time were crops of boils and I can still remember having a bottomful of the wretched things and trying to sit still on them for what seemed like an eternity, watching "*Mutiny on the Bounty*" at the old Radio Theatre in town. We were staying at a holiday cottage at the West End Beach at the time and this must have been the first movie I'd seen; certainly it was the first I remember. It was a Saturday afternoon matinee and we had seats in the very front row and a bit to the side so that one had almost to lie back to see anything. All the characters were long and thin and sprang about like a gaggle of animated fence posts! From this angle, the screen seemed to assume a slight forward tilt and for the full duration, I lived in dread that any moment the whole thing would come down on top of us in an unspeakable jumble of cursing, brawling mutineers and roistering sailormen. As for the long, thin kangaroo that hopped down at the beginning of the newsreel, I didn't dare to imagine where he might have ended up. So there I was, in mute agony, sitting as comfortably as the points of my boils would allow, stiff-necked from craning up and scared of what I'd see anyway, yet miserably aware that this was some kind of wonderful treat I was supposed to be enjoying.

Dad used to have boils badly at times too and once he had so many on the back of his neck that his head was immobilised and the pain must have been excruciating while poor Bob carried for years the scar of a monstrous, many-headed carbuncle in the bend of one elbow. I guess it could have been the sameness of our diet and the lack of fresh fruit that contributed to the cause, plus the fact that Dad in particular must have been rundown at times. Anyway, Mother treated us all alike with hot foments and tacky, black Bate's Salve which she melted over a candle flame before spreading onto clean rag and applying as a drawing agent, often having to pursue us around the kitchen table to put the dressing "in situ".

It was during the convalescent stages of our mumps, measles and chickenpox that the seeds of our later love of reading were sown. During the afternoons, instead of having a rest, Mother would come around to the sleepout and sit beside our iron beds and read to us for hours on end. And how the characters moved and lived and, alas, sometimes died as she applied her wonderful expression and interpretation to every page. Oh, how many tears we spilled for poor fretful, ill-starred Ginger in Anna Sewell's "*Black Beauty*". We learned the words by heart and the magnificent colour plates in every loving detail. Then there was "*Wild Horse Silver*", a little gem of a book set in the American West and with such lively pen sketches I can remember some of them to this day. She read us Banjo Paterson's book of verse, "*The Animals Noah Forgot*", Hans Andersen's stories, of which the "*Ugly Duckling*" was a firm favourite, mainly I think because of its happy ending. But happy ending or not, there must have been a good streak of melancholy in us as we revelled in a good cry.

Some of Grimm's Fairy Tales were popular and there was a thick, green volume of Bible stories called "*Line Upon Line*" which seemed fairly stern and joyless stuff. Being horse mad, the only part that interested me was where Elijah went up into the clouds in a fiery chariot drawn by horses-wonderful larger-than-life horses they were in the picture, with wild eyes and great sinewy haunches. Mother tried patiently to interest us in "*Peter Pan and Wendy*" but it was all so much beyond our ken that, though we listened and absorbed to some degree, it never became a favourite. For a start there were no horses and the idea of a dog being a nanny, a term we'd had no experience of anyway, was all too absurd. "*Alice in Wonderland*" suffered the same indifference. Talking rabbits and disappearing cats just weren't within the realms of possibility for us. Another book we had for years was "*Cole's Funny Book*" with a rainbow on the cover, but somehow I always felt a slight chill on opening it, as though peeping through the keyhole at someone else's discomfort and the humour seemed laborious. There was one picture of a row of boys in a whipping machine and all the childrens' faces looked grotesquely old and the adults so stern and mercilessly self-righteous that it just didn't seem to be a very funny book.

We were introduced to the world of Beatrix Potter and the Australian classics, "*Blinky Bill*" and "*Snugglepot and Cuddlepie*". Later we read for ourselves the Billabong books by Mary Grant Bruce and Owen Wister's unforgettable "*The Virginian*", "*The Story of an African Farm*" by Olive Schreiner and, in time, "*Gone with the Wind*" and many, many others. Ion Idriess was a favourite of Dad's and there was a growing collection of his works alongside those of Will Lawson, Frank Clune and Myrtle Rose White. In her own small desk, Mother had some books that fascinated me, though I never did more than feel them and look at the pictures. The one I remember best was a vellum-bound volume called "*Stories of the Opera*" with marvellously colourful pictures of a murderous-looking Carmen, swarthy and high cheek-boned with a rose between her teeth and a glitter in her eye.

Mother was a great little historian too, being especially interested in English history and able to relate the intricate details of lineage and events since William the Conqueror to anyone who'd sit still long enough to listen. Strangely, this didn't rub off on me until it was too late and how I was to regret it later when travelling and spending time in Europe, I felt at a loss to appreciate fully the historic value of many famous places. A good knowledge of history would have been an asset in Scotland too, where I lived for six months with a family in a big, draughty old hunting lodge on the banks of Loch Goil, not far from Dunoon on the west coast. Wonderful, wild country it was with pine forests on the mountain-sides and an earthy rawness in the air. The old lodge rang with the life and laughter of the four sturdy children I was employed to mind and my time there was entirely happy. With the three older ones, duffel coated and stockinged against the cutting wind, we walked for miles on the winding roads through the forests and on my weekly day off, I'd walk the several miles beside the tossing, chilly, grey loch to the cluster of white buildings that made up the village, huddled against the base of the mountain like eggs in a dark nest. There was always a little shopping to do, mail to post and collect and time to fill in yarning with the locals. Social life was unsophisticated and spontaneously enjoyed and my efforts at dancing an eightsome reel were generously applauded.

But I'm getting side-tracked, so back to childhood. Mother introduced us to religious instruction fairly early in our lives too, which was just as well as up till then, God had been an elderly, bearded gentleman in a cane chair, stationed somewhere in the sky above our house, and Hell was under the well near the cow paddock, deep and murky and peopled by gnarled and knobby banksia men who lurked there waiting for the unguarded to fall in. Her main source of guidance in this branch of our education was Miss Cecily Biddle, who was a deaconess in the

Church of England and whose many years of tireless work in the Bluff Point parish will long be remembered. Miss Biddle was a tall, spare lady with humorous eyes and a fringe of reddish hair that stuck out from under her short veil. She retained and used to effect her authoritative English accent and was undoubtedly regarded by many as an eccentric. We certainly giggled at her expense many time, but she was always interesting, always so full of enthusiasm and doing something and her devotion to God and his work, as she saw it, was monumental.

Always in the background, loyal and selfless, was "Nanna", her aged companion housekeeper, Miss Estwick. Nanna was a sweet-faced little lady with plaits around her head, very bright eyes behind round glasses and with a penchant for wearing dangly earrings that swung and jiggled with every movement. For some time, Sunday School classes were held in the Waggrakine school, but when that closed, they were held at our place on the fourth Sunday of every month. On these days, Miss Biddle's hump-backed old blue car would creep down our road, never out of second gear, and looking for all the world like some gargantuan mother beetle carrying her young on either side. Loaded to capacity inside with children she'd picked up along the way, there'd be several older ones standing on either side running board, laughing and chattering to each other as they hung on one-handed most of the time, a sight surely to send a modern day traffic inspector into a state of severe shock! But they were few and far between then and so the practice continued, perhaps by the grace of God, without accident, for several years.

After the lesson there'd be afternoon tea in the dining room for the grownups and we'd go out to play. We were generally pretty well-behaved, pottering about near the house, conscious of being in our good clothes and having to keep them clean. One afternoon, however, this routine didn't appeal much and David and I and a couple of boys who'd come over for the afternoon with their mother, drifted away from the others, followed by Bruno, the whippet, and Buster, a ginger jack-of-all-trades dog. Bruno was a fearless hunter despite his frail build and thin-skinned appearance and liked nothing better than a good chase. It wasn't long this day before we spotted the first rabbit and Bruno was off, yip-yipping as he flew after the doomed creature. After that there was no stopping him, or us. The pile of furry bodies grew and we were well pleased with ourselves as all country kids knew what a menace rabbits were and felt we'd done a good afternoon's work. I guess it was more a survival instinct than a blood lust; nothing cruel about it, just a quick, clean kill that we'd come to accept as a necessity. And yet I could no more kill a rabbit or anything else now than fly.

It wasn't till we heard a call from the house that we stopped to take a look at ourselves and each other. We were filthy! Buttons were missing along with my hair ribbon and there were jagged tears in socks and pants. Perhaps they'd be pleased if they saw what a good job we'd done, so we shared the catch and started back towards the house. What a spectacle! Miss Biddle had rounded up her charges and Mrs. Green was taking leave of Mother on the verandah as we hove into view. Three adult jaws dropped in unison at the sight of we who were supposed to be so full of sweetness and light and were now so thoroughly disreputable! The boys were bundled into their car without ceremony - minus rabbits - and David and I were shunted speechlessly off to the bathroom. No-one seemed very pleased at all with our good deed.

Another person who figured in our early religious-education was the Reverend K.B. Halley, later Canon Halley, who was then the Anglican minister in town. Once a week he'd come to school for scripture lessons, riding a bike or on foot - walking with his curiously long stride and flourishing a walking cane in front of him, up and down like a giant proboscis. At all times he wore a stiff-brimmed black hat and, in cooler weather, a voluminous black cape swung fore and aft and the effect was quite dramatic. Scripture lessons were never dull and we heard about all manner of things and places and happenings. Apart from his trips to school, Mr. Halley must have travelled miles around the town on his bike calling on parishioners at home or in hospital and taking communion to the elderly and those unable to attend church.

But one thing intrigued me more than anything else about him. At the end of each lesson he would look solemn, make a sign in the air and say something I simply couldn't make any sense of. Lesson after lesson I listened intently, peeping through my fingers to see which way his mouth went. But he spoke so quickly it was all over in a flash and I was none the wiser. So one night over the washing up, I asked, "Mother, why does Mr. Halley go like this at the end of every scripture lesson", I mimed the action, "and say 'blah, blah, blah - munching men of August?'" Mother leaned her soapy hands on the edge of the washing-up dish and asked incredulously, "He says what?" So the performance was repeated. After a moment's reflection Mother laughed so much it was some time before she could tell me that what Mr. Halley had been saying all that time was, "... be amongst you and remain with you always!" The "Munching Men of August" was a standard joke in our household for a long time after that. Perhaps the tendency to misinterpret may be an inherited weakness after all, as years later my own young son clasped his hands in earnest prayer and I heard to my private amusement, "Our Father, who aren't in Heaven ..."

CHAPTER 9

There was one thing we were never short of around the place and that was animal life. In lambing season, anything up to a dozen youngsters would be rescued after being abandoned by their mothers for some reason, and brought in at various stages to be raised. Milk was abundant, there were plenty of empty sauce and vinegar bottles and young hands to minister to them so we had a high success rate. Often the lambs were just pathetic little bundles of life with long, silky, knobby-kneed legs, needing plenty of patience and care and spending their first few nights in a box by the stove for warmth. Many a waif was to owe their survival to the warmth emanating from that old black stove over the years if they could have realised it. As they progressed they'd go out to a fenced-off area near the house until big and independent enough to re-join the mob. Each one had a name and there was Lambie and Sadsob and Clara and Rachel and so on and on.

If they survived those first early days and nights, the helpless stage was soon replaced, I might add, by a condition of persistent and rapacious hunger that was nearly impossible to satisfy. Bob and Margaret did the milking every day before school and it fell to Jenny and David and I to deal with the bunting, writhing, guzzling mass of lambs that sucked and nibbled at your knees, fingers or clothing and generally nearly bowled you over in an effort to be fed before their mates. They were always waiting for us and any movement outside the door around feed time would precipitate a deafening chorus of brassy voices, raised in protest. If the fence of the compound gave way under the weight of their enthusiasm, as sometimes happened, there'd be a stampede to the verandah where they'd stump about making puddles and scattering "pearls" whilst continuing their raucous demands outside a firmly shut door.

Jenny and I had our special pets, in this case a pair of crossbred wether lambs, Larry and Charlie. Petted and pampered and as fat as butter, they nevertheless had to put up with the occupational hazards of being "pet" lambs and submitted with fair grace to wearing string bridles and bits of improvised harness and pulling a little billy cart which they invariably bolted with. We were very sad when the time came for them to go out with the mob and were quite sure they'd never survive without us to care for them. However, apart from coming up to renew acquaintances every time they were yarded with the rest of the sheep, they never looked like pining for their protected existence and thrived till a ripe old age on their own initiative.

For a brief, hectic interlude there was a kid someone gave us and we called him simply, Mr. Goat. He was quite adorable with his silky black and white coat and quizzical tan dots for eyebrows but managed to cram more misdeeds into a few months than most goats would hope for in a lifetime.

Nothing was sacred. He ate Mother's spinach and nasturtiums with as much gusto as the few Iceland poppies she had managed to nurture tenderly by hand watering and chewed the crown out of Dad's new straw harvester hat as he sat on the side verandah one day, having a cup of tea. Even for one of his nimble species, Mr. Goat seemed to have an over-developed passion for leaping and springing onto high levels, and this was to cause more than one mad progress through the house. Several times he slipped the dog collar he wore on his neck or chewed through the rope we tethered him with and, on each occasion, made a beeline for the open back door of the kitchen. The dogs would see him coming and, looking for a bit of sport with this strange sheep-like animal they had never become truly reconciled to having about the place, would rush out and bark at him.

This terrified poor Mr. Goat, who was really quite small and defenceless and decidedly peace-loving and he'd put on a tremendous burst of speed to get in the door before being overtaken by dogs. Scared out of his wits by now, he'd hurtle into the kitchen, skidding wildly on the pot-holed cement floor, trailing a portion of frayed rope behind him and closely followed by several furiously barking sheep dogs! His one aim after that was to jump as high and as often as he could to escape them, so the mad procession tore from one room to the next, Mr. Goat springing and bleating in terror from bed to bed to dressing table while we kids, helpless with laughter, plunged after them all, trying desperately to grab the rope and tripping over the dogs and each other and everything in the way.

Once, after completing the circuit of dining room and bedrooms without being rescued, he doubled back and skidded into the kitchen, leaping onto the shelf of the kitchen dresser, knocking over a china jug and the alarm clock, both of which promptly smashed. The whole crazy exercise had been completed so rapidly that Mother had hardly had time to move from the stove where she had been stirring something. Mr. Goat's next move was a great bound onto the smaller of the two kitchen tables where a big green dish of scalded milk was set to cool, prior to being skimmed. In his panic he made a neat if ill-judged landing with both front feet in the milk. That was his undoing. They shot from under him and he came down half in the bowl, slopping milk and cream onto the floor. Mother grabbed him before he could escape to run riot again and speechlessly handed him over to us to take and put him in his night yard. With the excitement over, the dogs went back under the trees and we left Mr. Goat to lick the milk from his legs and ponder the error of his ways before going reluctantly back to face Mother.

That was definitely it. He'd have to go!

"Oh, but Mother, it wasn't his fault. He didn't mean to. The dogs scared him!" It was safe to blame the dogs as they couldn't be got rid of.

"Please Mother. We'll put him on a chain next time then he won't be able to chew through it. It wasn't his fault, Mother - truly. He didn't mean to."

And so Mr. Goat had another chance and for a few peaceful weeks he munched and chomped over in the ram paddock, twitching his quizzical eyebrows and rattling his chain, with an eye on the back door of the kitchen all the while. Then, one Sunday afternoon we had visitors. Mother sat at the big oval table in the dining room and poured tea from the silver teapot that had been polished to brilliance for the occasion. We were all in our Sunday clothes and there was a bowl of flowers in the centre of the table amongst the scones and cakes and best glass cups. We didn't know the people very well at this stage but conversation was flowing smoothly and politely enough to make everyone feel comfortable.

Suddenly the dogs began to bark. No-one took much notice at first and then it was too late. Seconds later there was a familiar panic-stricken bleating, a sound of dragging metal and then a scamper of tiny hooves on the three wooden steps that led up to the back door. One of us rushed to slam it - in time at least to shut the dogs out but not quickly enough to halt the whirlwind entry of Mr. Goat. With the grace of a ballerina and the quickness of a cat, he landed on the table before a hand could be lifted to stop him. In a second he'd wrenched the flowers from their vase and stood balefully surveying the speechless company, his mouth crammed and water dripping from the foolishly protruding stalks! Shock was the universal reaction. No-one moved or spoke at first and after all, what could be said.

This really was the limit. Whether he meant to or not, this was it! Poor Mother was nearly in tears. Though we were to laugh with our friends about it in years to come, then it was disgraceful. The rest of the surroundings were shabby enough without having a goat mixed up with the afternoon tea. We knew Mr. Goat's number was up and there could be no argument. One day not long after this episode, we came home to find he'd gone. Dad said he'd given him to one of the shearers who was working there at the time and we left it at that. Life was certainly more peaceful without him, but what child wants a peaceful life forever?

We three younger ones now turned our attention back to the cats to help pass some of the time on weekends and holidays. Dolls or any kind of toys were so scarce as to be rare. There was one aged rabbit, almost completely hairless from handling, that had been passed right down the line, a couple of teddy bears - one of which had pink eyes and had a nose badly disfigured by Bob persistently sucking it as a small boy - an unrealistic-looking celluloid doll, and that was about it. So all the cats endured turns at being pressed into a rickety cane pram and wheeled about like babies after taking feeds with great reluctance and suspicion from a lamb's feeding bottle. It was quite hilarious to see tabby Clarence with his handsome white bib and paws, bobbing about in the pram with a perfectly asinine expression on his face. Why he didn't spring out and take to the bush and stay there I'll never know. Perhaps this was a small price to pay for plenty of fresh meat and milk and wide, cool verandahs to lie on in the heat of the day.

Once a zealous Salvation Army man, having pedalled his bike out from town and down our dusty road, parked it under a tree and lifted his hand to knock at the kitchen door. His eyes popped in disbelief at the two strange figures that shot between his feet as he stood there. A wild-eyed, exasperated Precious, with an old baby's bonnet slung rakishly under one ear, followed hotly by Clarence, his hind paws scrabbling furiously to get a hold on the cement floor through a trailing petticoat, made their exit. The poor man must have though he'd been at least mildly affected by the sun but was reassured by Mother over a cup of tea before he left to resume his daunting mission: daunting, not only for the one mode of transport available to him, but because, with all the goodwill in the world, there couldn't have been much to collect for all his pedalling.

The first cat I remember and the patriarch of the clan was a huge old tabby tom called Pretty Man. He was deposed by a handsome ginger we called Oomprow - that was the closest we could get to the sound of his call. Oomprow lived in the creek and made only rare and furtive appearances near the house. It was his throaty night calls that caused me as a young child to lie awake, staring into the dark, half expecting to see a shadowy form slip stealthily in the open sleepout door. If one of the others were awake they'd say sleepily by way of reassurance, "It's only a tomcat". But my mental picture of a tomcat was far from reassuring; a great long-legged feline with a face as big and round as a dinner plate and with short, scarred ears almost hidden in stiff fur. They were always ginger and stood about two feet high! What a relief it was to realise eventually that tomcats were perfectly ordinary and familiar man cats.

The most memorable of all the cats that came and went during my childhood was a dark tortoise-shell kitten that strayed in one cold, wet night during the middle war years, just before Grandpa died in fact, surveyed us all through her blazing amber eyes and decided she preferred our company to the storm outside. The last thing we needed was another cat - especially a female of the species - but Mother would have been the last person in the world to deny a waif, so she was fed and feted and naturally stayed - for about fifteen years.

We named her various names but the one that stuck was Bergman - after Ingrid Bergman whom we'd so admired in an early Photoplay movie magazine. They were both good-looking and they had class. Our Bergman, when she reached maturity, produced batches of kittens with monotonous regularity - fluffy little tabbies and gingers and blacks and some of her own dark tortoise-shell. And after every batch Mother would say, "Stuart, you really must get rid of that cat before she has more kittens!" And Dad would agree: yes, he really must. But somehow Bergman beat them to it every time and as she swelled prior to the next clutch, there could be no question of "putting the poor thing out to fend for herself". I had a shrewd notion though, that Bergman could have fended very well for herself under any conditions, as she not only had class, but was a battler of heroic proportions. Many's the time she toiled home, an almost comic sight, head straining up high and front legs straddling the limp body of a hapless rabbit, often nearly as big as herself. She'd fling the victim down defiantly on the verandah and stalk off as if to say to her waiting brood, "There you are. I've done the best I can for you!"

Bergman survived epidemics of cat flu that laid low many of her offspring and contemporaries, misadventures with several rabbit traps and a fall down a well. Once when she lay in the shade of the creeper for days and nights on end, too sick and feeble to move or be moved, we thought it really was the end -

probably the result of eating a poisoned rabbit - and our efforts to save her were infinitely tender. At last life flickered and stirred and rallied again. So there were more kittens and threats of deportation and rabbits on the verandah and all was as before. Her final effort was one ginger tom kitten, then a little peace to lie in the sun and enjoy old age before she simply disappeared, going back to the bush to die.

CHAPTER 10

During this time the war was raging on and on and farm hands were impossible to hire. It would have been quite beyond our means to pay anyone a wage anyway, so naturally, as they grew up, Bob and Margaret took on more and more of the farm work. So much so that Dad had several visits from inspectors querying the gaps in their school attendance. Margaret was nearly seven years my senior and by the time she was thirteen, she was as adept at handling horses as any man that came on to the place. Apart from Grandpa, it was generally she whom I remember taking the reins on any driving excursions around the farm. A horseman born and bred, she was game to try anything where horses were involved, whether riding or driving and managed a team of eight in the Sunderseeder with as much aplomb as a pair or team of four in the wagon. This wagon which I've mentioned so often, was a source of pride to us as it had begun its career as a truck tray and was fitted with pneumatic tyres and a hand-brake which seemed remarkably sophisticated. Certainly it was, compared to the great archaic, iron-wheeled dray which stood idle by the chaff house, unused since the last of the scrub clearing. Years before that, before our time too, Dad had jolted over the unmade road to town with loads of rocks on board the dray for the breakwater off the West End beach at Geraldton. And on one nightmare journey, he'd been prostrated on top of his flinty cargo, writhing with acute appendicitis and had "just made it" to the hospital.

Mother, a town person herself, and generally fully occupied in the house anyway, often seemed insulated in her own little world of thought and couldn't have been aware of all the risks that Margaret in particular was exposed to or, like poor Marie Antoinette, she would have gone grey overnight with worry. I think for the most part she was blissfully unaware of all the things that could have gone wrong but fortunately almost never did.

Carting water was a constant chore throughout our childhood and until there was a reliable supply laid onto the house, which wasn't until the later war years, it had to be brought - per wagon - from various soaks and dams and for a while from the public tanks about six miles from home. Bob and Margaret, when they were reckoned to be old enough, would be dispatched on these excursions, she driving and he as an outrider. Along the way they'd be joined by Francis and Graham and anyone else at a loose end and with a bike. The trip down to the tanks was invariably sedate: the horses were subdued at the idea of going away from home and it was often hot. But the desire to liven things up a bit on the return journey overwhelmed the entire convoy and who could blame them? It was a long, slow plod made in the heat of the day and they were only youngsters.

Once the tanks were filled, the two horses quickened their step as their heads were turned for home and so they started back with brimming tanks and lifted hearts. One of the tanks had no lid and, in an effort to stabilise the water and prevent some of the slop, pieces of board were floated on top of it. This measure could have been mildly effective if Dad's strict injunctions not to go above a walk, not even to jog, had been observed. But the last mile home is the longest and once off the main road and inside the Mail Gate, such restrictions were cast to the four winds and there was always a fair amount of spillage from the open tank.

Going out for the day with the team — Mother and all.

One day, however, there was more than usual. The horses were pulling hard by the time they were through the gate, harder than usual, and they were excited and eager to get home. There were cries of "Beat cha!" from the bike riders that couldn't be ignored and so they were off, trotting at first, with Margaret doing her best to hold them in. But they were big, strong brutes with the scent of home in their nostrils and their strength was more than a match for hers. Soon they were at a smart canter with their lightweight driver almost standing on the wagon pole, hauling with all her strength on the reins but making little impression on their iron will. With every jolt and bump on that jolting, bumping road, precious water slopped and sloshed all over the wagon, saturating the bagging laid under the tanks and losing itself in a thin trail on the dusty track. Like some grotesque and clumsy Roman chariot they lumbered down the last stretch of road, Margaret fortunate enough to be able to hang on herself, let alone give a thought to the water in the open tank or any other! With one last huge effort and some measure of exhaustion on the horses' behalf, she managed to haul them up just out of sight of the house and make a fairly sedate entry on the home scene. But there was no need to explain to Dad the nearly empty tank as he silently surveyed the sweating horses, drenched wagon and trembling driver. It had been a close call for her.

This background must account at least in part for what amounts to almost a fixation with me about water wastage. Remembering those youngsters toiling backwards and forwards in the heat and later having a small part in it myself, an abundance of good water seems to me to be a gift from God and its availability is not to be abused or taken for granted. After all, wherever in the world there is none, there are deserts and where there is little, there is harshness and privation. Many the time my long-suffering family has had to restrain me from springing out of the car to turn off taps and sprinklers where water seems to be running to waste. There are cries of, "Oh, Mum! It's none of your business!" But I can't help feeling that it is.

Bob — more at home with the tractor than horsepower.

* * *

I've said before that Dad could be a pretty hard task master and there was at least one occasion when we felt there was a certain amount of poetic justice in a small misfortune that befell him. They were scooping out a fresh waterhole in the creek for the stock to drink at and the kids had been having a fairly torrid time of it. Bob, in his early teens, wrestled manfully with the heavy dam scoop while Dad directed operations from the bank in stentorian tones and using his own particularly picturesque style of dialogue. Margaret, a year older than Bob, but weighing scarcely seven stone at that stage, was hard put to control the four draught horses in the scoop which were thoroughly stirred up with all the ballyhoo, continually rushing the far bank of the creek and getting further off course each time they made a run at it.

They were all feeling the strain by the time Jenny, David and I walked up from the houses carrying a billy of hot tea and thick jam sandwiches for morning tea. Everyone eased themselves gratefully to the ground, propping aching backs against handy wattle bushes and took their share of the refreshment, munching in silence. The horses too stood quietly now, as glad as anyone of the break, heads down and tails swishing idly at the odd bothersome fly. No-one spoke and all was quiet and still.

Suddenly there was a muffled shout from Dad as he sprang to his feet, clutching his throat. We watched in astonished silence as he pranced about, stopping to gulp a mouthful of hot tea before grabbing his throat again. There followed a series of violent and explosive hawks and spits and on about the fourth hawk, just as he was reaching desperation point, out shot a very bedraggled and half-cooked bull ant, followed by quite an impressive spot of blood! Apparently the ant had a sweet tooth too and fancied some of Dad's sandwich. When it had been put on the ground for a moment, he'd taken the opportunity to bury himself between the two layers of bread, all the better to get at the jam in the centre. However, when the time came, he was not to be bustled so unceremoniously on a journey through the dark interior, so grabbed a tonsil as he went by and hung on for dear life! Bob and Margaret both felt great justification for their lack of sympathy and Dad was much chastened. The rest of the scooping operation was directed in a hoarse croak when not in silence - and with a minimum of drama.

* * *

There was yet another job that Margaret relieved Dad at as she grew older and that was driving the poison cart. This was for laying poison baits for the multitudes of rabbits that farmers then seemed to wage ceaseless and seemingly ineffectual wars against. The cart itself, looking like a pre-historic edition of a trotting spider, was a two-wheeled affair and had a plough seat fitted for the driver to sit on and a funnel underneath for the baits to come out of. There was a disc to cut a shallow furrow for them to fall into, and as I remember it, a weight was put on top of the cylinder containing the mixture to force it down and a chain drove the chopper that cut the baits to a regulated size. This chopper had to be watched to see that it didn't jam and as the driver couldn't see what was going on under the cart, there always had to be a rider alongside to keep an eye on it and make sure the baits were coming out at regular intervals.

There was nothing haphazard about this poisoning business; the machinery, simple as it was, had to work, the baits had to be the right size and poisoning was always done late on a hot day. The moisture in the mixture attracted the rabbits then and these conditions enhanced the smell of the aniseed which was added to the bran, pollard and phosphorous-based poison. Dad would never let us get very close to the cart when he was mixing or handling the poison but I can remember watching from a distance and seeing the damp mixture fuming as the phosphorous was added and the smell was not unpleasant.

Poor Margaret, she hated driving that wretched cart. Apart from the fact that it was iron-tyred and unsprung, it had, of necessity, to be taken out on hot days at no more than walking pace for mile on mile, often over very rough country. So the outrider, or riders, were as necessary for company as anything else. To make the job more hateful, all stock had to be taken out of the paddocks that were to be poisoned and before they could be returned, any baits still lying in the furrow had to be picked up. This had to be done on foot as there could be no chance of any being missed. So all in all, it was a tiresome job and no-one enjoyed poisoning the rabbits anyway. Like fumigating the burrows and trapping, it was a harsh measure, done for simple survival.

* * *

It wasn't only with horses that Margaret's flair for stock work lay. This good-natured, long-legged kid with the merry brown eyes and thick auburn plaits, seemed to have inherited all of old Joshua's instinct for sheep as well and came to be an expert in her knowledge in every department of their management. We all had to do our bit with the work as I've said before but it was with Margaret that Dad conferred on any subject where he felt he needed a second opinion. She learned from him too, the art of wool classing as Dad had attended a course on the subject at one of the big mills in the north of England between the end of the war and coming back to Australia so was fairly well versed and she, as always, was a quick and willing pupil.

In fact, many years further on, as an Adelaide housewife with four under school-age children "at foot", she was to observe wistfully one day when things were more than usually chaotic, "Oh well, I don't suppose there are many housewives around here who could drive an eight horse team or class a wool clip!" And I'm sure there weren't.

Shearing was always a very busy time for Dad and Mother and an exciting one for we youngsters with all the activity and bustle that overtook the usual routine. Shearers coming to work at our place in those days brought their own plant as we had none and Dad had had to borrow a neighbour's for the soldier shearers who came to help out. The men stayed on the job during the week, sleeping in a small room not far from the house. They used our bathroom, such as it was, and had all meals with us, going home on the weekend if they were local men. With two or three extras to cook for three times a day plus morning and afternoon smokos and school lunches as well, Mother's catering resources must have been taxed to the limit. And she had no extra help, apart from us girls when she could keep us for long enough, to cope with the mountains of greasy pots and boilers and dishes.

That was bad enough but perhaps most trying was deciding "what to have". There was rarely anything but mutton which must have simplified things a bit but the eternal question was what to do with it. I hate to think back on the battle she must have had to keep the uncooked meat fresh as we certainly didn't always have a refrigerator, only a flywired meat safe that stood on the side verandah catching any breeze that blew and had its feet in jam tins full of water to discourage ants from climbing into it. I say "discourage" as this measure certainly didn't always prevent and I've seen that safe a seething mass of ants after dust formed a scum on the water in one of the tins or a piece of straw or grass lay on the top, forming a minute bridge for the little creatures to cross over in their voracious determination; and I suppose like us they were always hungry. Down in a rickety bough shed, loosely termed the "meat house", the freshly slaughtered carcase was strung up in several clean chaff bags to swing in the breeze and keep as cool as possible before being cut up and put in the meat safe.

There was a large chopping block in the meat house and one blow from Dad's cleaver would precipitate a stampede of cats that had to be seen to be believed! They came from everywhere, tails stuck upright like little flagpoles and quivering with excitement and anticipation. It was comical to see Dad's antics as he chopped and cleaved doggedly on to the accompaniment of all those frantic feline voices as they clutched and clawed and clung to his trouser legs, letting out an occasional screech as paws and tails were trodden on in the rush.

Back in the kitchen, there was always "pudding" at night, shearing time or not, and with a good supply of eggs and milk, this was not so much of a problem as the meat course. Rice pudding, when rice was available, and bread and butter pudding have never tasted so good. There were thin, sweet yellow custards and jellies and junkets that had to be painstakingly placed for hours in any available breeze to set and stewed prunes and dried apricots and "jack apples" that came in bulk quantities and had to be hidden away or were relentlessly plundered by us all. These stores were delivered monthly on the Yuna mail truck and just sometimes, as a special treat, we'd find at the bottom of the big, splintery crate, a lumpy, knobbly parcel of a couple of pounds of boiled lollies and then our joy was complete.

Often it was hot around shearing time and the kitchen was an inferno with the stove stoked well all day for cooking and keeping water boiling for tea and washing up. Flies, attracted from miles around by the permanent smell of something going on, zoomed in through the open doors in droves in a frenzy of perpetual excitement. Many of them came to grief on the sticky fly papers that spiralled languidly from the ceiling or were spread out in large, flat squares on the table between meals. Like the ever present rabbits and the trannies in the dub and sleepout, the flies were an accepted part of our childhood, especially at shearing time. I don't recall any of us becoming ill as a direct result of the flies even though they were maddening and unpleasant, but I do wonder at the reaction a single fly can produce in some people today. He's likely to find himself pursued to the death kick with copious blasts from a pressure can of spray, that fills the air and contains goodness knows what that was never intended for inhalation by human beings. I do wonder which is more harmful to our over-civilised systems the fly or the spray!

Margaret and Bob quite often missed school to help in the shed and muster for shearing and we three younger ones were always delighted when weekends or holidays coincided with it too. Then we did our share of mustering and returning shorn sheep to their home paddocks and ho!hoing! in the dusty sheep yards in a welter of barking dogs and wildly waving arms. But the highlight of the days came at smokos. At the sound of Mother's bell, two of us went scuttling back to the house to get the billies of scalding tea and food and enamel mugs that were strung together on twine for easy carrying. Back in the shed the two stand plant would putter to a stop and everyone eased themselves down into a pile of wool, mug in one hand, eats in the other.

With the engine idle, the shed was strangely silent; the only sound from the sheep in the holding pens was the rattle of "pearls" through the slatted wooden floors and the occasional snort or grinding of teeth as they waited their turn to cross the board, emerging absurdly naked to skid down the shute into the counting-out pen outside. The air was heavy with the smell of wool and lanolin and tar and it was a great time for telling yarns and good-natured ribbing and I listened with near reverence to these sweaty gods in greasy dungarees and laughed willingly at all their jokes and riddles, their tall stories and anecdotes. There was a brain teaser that came up year after year and was always trotted out if there was someone new to try it on: "Sisters and brothers I have none, but that man's father is my father's son". Many an argument and discussion was provoked by that in its time but it was all good fun and soon enough it was time to take a last pull on a smoke, oil hand-pieces and start the engine for the next "run".

Before we took the tea things back to the house, there'd be catching pens to fill and wool to be pressed, with us jumping and tramping on "pieces" and "bellies" in two bales held upright from the shed rafters by wire. Bob worked on the main wool press while Margaret picked up the fleeces and kept the board clear and acted as "tar boy" where necessary. Dad kept an eye everywhere and directed operations from the big wool table where he skirted and classed the fleeces as Margaret flung them out. No-one stood idle or had time to wonder what to do next. Once back at the house with the mugs and billies, my main thought would be to escape again as soon as possible to the noise and bustle of the shed; brat that I was, my domestic chores were done only grudgingly as they seemed so dull compared to what was going on elsewhere. It was automatic that we all helped with washing up after meals, especially at night, but anything much beyond that brought wails of protest from me at least. Jenny was far more domesticated and helpful, which was as well for Mother, as she needed an ally in the camp.

At knock off time, there were shorn sheep to be returned to their paddocks, often quite a distance from home, the shed to be filled with sheep for the next day and cows to be milked, so we were all tired by tea time. This was the most leisurely meal of the day as it was cooler by now and everyone more relaxed with the pressure off until the following morning. The men came up from their room at the sound of the cowbell with hair slicked back and clean clothes replacing the grey flannel sweat shirts and greasy dungarees they'd worn during the day and after tea, stayed a while to listen to the radio or play cards with us around the kitchen table before retiring for the night. They were long, busy days for all but as Dad loved to quote in his more philosophical moods from Gordon's "Sick Stock Rider", "The hardest day was never then too hard".

CHAPTER 11

Things started to improve for us financially in the later war years although we didn't see much result of it immediately, the first year's good income going entirely to repay long-standing debts to the Bank and Stock Firms. Then, little improvements that had been previously quite beyond our means, started gradually to become realities. The first of these would have been a water supply to the house from a soak over in the Ram Paddock.

There had always been a big, damp patch there and Dad sometimes grew a few melons and pumpkins around it. When the rams were in residence, nothing would persuade Jenny and me to go across to the garden as one night a particularly mean-minded Dorset Horn ram called Hitler, had bowled Margaret over as she came in the direction of home with her arms full of Queensland Blues and Ironbarks, catching her from behind and sending pumpkins in all directions. He was coming at her again but she was quick enough to scramble to her feet in time to snatch up a hefty Ironbark and bounce it off the astonished animal's skull, sending him off shaking his head and licking his lips and probably slightly concussed! After that I kept well clear - for fear of Hitler.

There were just two water points put on to the house, one a great big tap that still stands at the corner of the remaining section of verandah, outside where the kitchen door used to be, the other to the shower in the bathroom. For the first time, now there was water enough to cultivate a patch of lawn where there had always just been bare dirt and Mother could have something in the garden other than sunflowers and jade and statice. So there were citrus trees and cape gooseberries and pansies and a number of other vegetable crops and annuals she'd never been able to have before. This supply was only for house and garden, though, and was not unlimited so we still had to be careful in our useage and kept the rainwater in the big tank at the back for drinking and hair rinsing. Mint flourished under the tank stand, dark and sweet-smelling in the cool sand and nearby, a bush Mother called a moonflower gave off heady perfume at night.

In time there was a reasonable harness shed too and the saddles had gone from the side verandah and kitchen. Another improvement long overdue was the lining of the sleepout walls with white plasterboard which was a major undertaking involving us all in some way. I remember we did it during one Christmas holiday when, as usual, it was hot. Tempers were beginning to wear thin before we were far advanced. Dad balanced on a box, his hammer poised and mouth bristling with nails, ready to strike as soon as we had the board in place. But that was easier said than done! Several of us were equipped with brooms and mops to hold the sheets of plasterboard up. Our task was not made easier by the fact that the board was pretty heavy, also, to avoid marking its pristine whiteness, we had clean rags tied around the broom and mop heads, making them slip and lose their grip on the smooth surface. The sheets wobbled hectically until nailed firmly in place and we were all mighty tired in the shoulders and arms by the time it was done, but we knew it had been well worth the effort as we stood back to admire the effect after the last nail had been driven into the last batten. The shabby old sleepout had been magically transformed! And now there was something to hang pictures on - as long as we drove the tacks into the battens and not the plasterboard. Many a time after that I went around the verandah to look in at the sleepout door just for the pure joy of seeing it look so nice. The cement floor was still rough and uncovered and cruelly cold to bare feet first thing on a winter morning but oh! - the beauty of those crisp white walls in place of corrugated iron or the tattered hessian lining which was all we'd ever had before.

In time, even outdoor washdays were almost a thing of the past. I say "almost" as our new washhouse that stood down under the gum trees, had three walls and a roof but was completely open at the front. Perhaps Mother would have felt claustrophobic anyway if fully enclosed, after all those years "al fresco", and just to make her feel at home, the gum nuts that used to plop into the tubs and copper, now rattled on the iron roof as they fell from the trees. There were two stone wash troughs replacing the galvanised tubs and a window above them opened to give a view of the creek. The copper was still stoked for hot water for washing and bathing and the wash-house site remained a meeting place and stopping-off point on the way to the house.

But the thing that was to make the biggest difference to the routine was Mr. Simpson, the brand new washing machine that stood in the washhouse and, when not in use, was draped and covered with protective wraps to keep out the dust and elements that blew in the open front of the small building. Mr. Simpson was powered by a small petrol motor and was to belt and slosh his way through tons of Mills washing, rendering obsolete the washboard and to some extent, the copper. This really was a step forward after all the energy expended in rubbing and scrubbing and wringing and hauling in and out of the copper and I don't believe the novelty ever truly wore off that first washing machine. We all learned how to use it so, when the family was around, washday retained its "social" atmosphere with all and sundry helping to get the job done.

Our old original black radio had been replaced now by a slightly more modern, upright model and, as far as entertainment went, for a good number of years, the weekly high spot in our TV-less world where outings were rare and luxuries were still limited to say the least, was Saturday night with genial Harry Atkinson on Radio 6GE, Geraldton. Homework, always easily overlooked, was abandoned altogether on Saturday night and the chores were done with alacrity so that everyone could be gathered around the radio in time to hear the first segment of "Music Magazine of the Air". This was Hillbilly Roundup, and was the favourite part of the whole evening, for most of we youngsters at least.

Several of us crowded into or perched on Dad's big armchair, or, if he was using it, dragged others up to the radio end of the dining room. Mother sat on her small sofa in the far corner of the long room, bathed in a pool of light shed by the tall lamp which stood on the china cupboard. Sometimes as she listened to or quietly observed — almost like a spectator — her noisy, roistering brood, she must have wondered how she ever managed to produce such a bunch of rudely healthy, voluble creatures. Not that she and Dad weren't blessed with good health; they were, but neither were great talkers and Dad for one, found "small talk" as he called it, quite beyond his interest or capabilities. It was tacitly agreed, I believe, that it was the Maley in us that caused the gregariousness and rumpus!

At last we were settled and quiet and as Mother watched us, her hands were never idle. There was always a pile of mending to get through and only in the heat of summer did she not have knitting on the needles for one of us. And always, always there were socks to darn. Many a lamplit evening was spent endlessly pulling grass-seeds out of hairy woollen work-socks before darning them.

On unbearably hot nights, we'd sit just outside the dining room door on the verandah and listen from there and it was on nights like these that bugs and moths and hard-backed beetles buzzed and flapped in the open door, attracted by the lamp and seemingly bent on a fiery and dramatic death. Sometimes, when the wick was out of adjustment, the frail mantle would blaze and there were cries of "Mother, Mother! The lamp's on fire!" and she'd calmly adjust it before we settled to listen again. But best of all were the cold or rainy nights when we'd gather as close as we could to the kitchen stove, warming our feet and hands. There was hot cocoa for everyone and we'd all be armed with fence wire forks for making toast on the glowing coals. Radios weren't portable then so we couldn't take it to the kitchen with us, but turned up the volume so as not to miss anything above the chatter and general activity.

Time and time again we heard the same old favourites requested in the Hillbilly section: "Deep in the Heart of Texas", "The Strawberry Roan", "Boy, How She Could Yodel", and "The Bridle Hangin' on the Wall", to name but a few. Some of the more lugubrious strains were "The Drover's Wife", "The Face on the Barroom Floor", "The Letter Edged in Black", and who could forget Will Carter's mournful "Put My Little Shoes Away". My own personal heroes were Hank Snow, Tex Moreton, Gene Autrey and Reg Lindsay and "The Sons of the Pioneers" were unforgettable to me as they sang "A Penny for your Thoughts" or in fact anything else. As time went on a very young-sounding Slim Dusty came over the airwaves with "Rusty, It's Goodbye", "When the Rain Tumbles Down in July" and the heart-stoppingly nostalgic "When its Lamplighting Time in the Valley". It was fun too hearing school friends' requests being read out. One of my pals regularly requested "Old Shep", a la Tex Moreton and just as regularly had to retire to bed early, overcome by grief for poor Shep and his fate.

The next half hour of the programme was "Old Time Favourites" and we thrilled to John Charles Thomas' robust "Open Road, Open Sky" and grew to memorise by heart every beat of "The Christian Waltz" and "The Dancing Pennies" and many others, most of them never heard now. Modern Favourites was about as close as we could get to the pop scene of the time and there was "Johnny Zero" and "Coming in on a Wing and a Prayer" to remind us that it was still wartime. Vera Lynn was popular as was Gracie Fields. One of the songs I remember best from around that time was "My Dreams Are Getting Better All The Time" and perhaps it was later that we first heard "Harriet with a Lariat". There was a bit of fun too with Reginald Gardner's "Trains" and "Laughing Gas" by Cicely Courtenage had us in fits no matter how many times we heard it in the Comedy Section, likewise "Motoring" or "A Day at the Office" by Harry Tate.

These were great days for radio and radio fans, and I guess it's hard for modern children to realise just how much we relied on it for entertainment; also I believe there was a kind of intimacy about radio that is quite missing from television, like reading the book instead of just seeing the picture. Many of the shows were lighthearted, like "Fred and Maggie", which we all agreed was "silly", but like "Green Bottle", wouldn't miss and we couldn't help laughing at Roy Rene "Mo", though Mother was sure he was "a common little man". Jack Davey was popular and many an entertainer had their beginnings on Amateur Hour. Through the medium of radio too, the public was exhorted to invest in Bonds, avoid over-spending and watch out at all times for the Squander Bug who lay in wait for the improvident and appeared in the local paper as a small gremlin-like figure with a huge mouth, forked tail and skinny legs. The adults listened to the News with what amounted almost to reverence, but to us children, Saturday night was a weekly highlight and was to remain so for a number of years.

* * *

As far as providing our own musical entertainment went, regrettably none of us ever learned to master a musical instrument. For a while Bob plucked tentatively on something he called a banjo-mandolin and he could knock out a reasonable tune on a harmonica, but that was about as far as it went. Mother, who'd been something of a classical pianist herself, used to say she wished Jenny could have had piano lessons, but it couldn't be fitted into our long school day and bus schedule, and there was no car for weekend trips to town, so it remained an unfulfilled ideal.

Mother had had her own piano but with a young family there wasn't much time for such relaxation and over the years her fingers stiffened from lack of practice. While Grandpa had been alive there was no question of anyone practising anyway as the sound went straight through the unlined, uninsulated walls and a few chords would have the old man shouting, "Stop that racket! Stop that racket!" So, for the sake of precious domestic harmony, and because the piano was unused and untuned and deteriorating because of it, Mother decided to sell while it was still worth something. No doubt the money was desperately needed anyway. I can dimly remember as a small child, standing on the verandah with Mother, holding her hand one day, watching the piano out of sight as it went up the road in a cart behind someone else's big grey horse that looked just like our old Prince. Lord knows the memories and hopes and aspirations that left with it that day. All I know is that we stood watching for a long time.

None of us were gifted with any volume of singing voice either, though we all loved music and I for one feel profound regret at this thoughtless oversight of nature. Of all God's gifts, it seems to me a good singing voice must surely be one of the most pleasurable assets one could possess. Mother had quite a pretty voice in a light way and often used to sing at her work. There was one little song in particular that I've never heard since those days and was one of her favourites:

"Out on the mesa, bright stars above me,
I ride across the plain, I'm coming home again
Hoping, believing, that you still love me
For I am on my way, to you my Adele."

Dad, by contrast, had plenty of deep voice but, to use his own turn of phrase, had about as much idea of melody as "a bear on a drum"! He told us that when he was a small boy, there'd apparently been a degree of desirability about at least appearing "musical", by way of having suitably tapered fingers. His mother used to encourage him daily to spend a few minutes pinching the tips of his fingers, vainly attempting to promote the effect she so longed for in her robust and impossibly unmusical only son. Poor Hannah, doting mother that she was, even she must have seen what an impossible task it was with those big, strong, square-tipped fingers that were never meant to be anything else. Certainly, for all the pinching that went on in childhood, the effect later was negligible - but Hannah didn't live to see that, as she died when he was still only a child.

During our school years there were a couple of runaways that broke the routine and gave us something to talk about for a while; the first put Margaret in direct peril of her life and the second was a close thing for almost the whole family. David and I were playing about on the verandah one day, probably driving the cats mad, when he happened to glance up towards the Clover Paddock where Dad and Margaret were finishing a bit of seeding with the team. Suddenly there was a shout of more amusement than alarm, "Mother, come and look at the horses! They look funny with their white faces all going up and down. Quick!" David called again before Mother and Jenny came out from whatever they were doing inside to look up to where he was pointing. And, sure enough, their white faces did look funny all going up and down; they were going flat out in a mad bolt down the paddock with the Sunderseeder careering along crazily behind!

Poor Mother, her heart must have been in her throat as she ran to the edge of the verandah, quite powerless to do anything but watch the little drama. As we stood there hardly daring to look for fear of what might happen in front of our very eyes, the horses began to turn, gradually describing a wide curve and we could see a lone, slender figure on the plank of the cumbersome machine. A huge dark shower of damp earth flared out from the discs as they made their turn and the harrows bounded wildly behind. As an extra load came on them with the uphill turn, they began to slow down until at last, after what seemed like an eternity, they were still, coming to a halt with sides foaming and mouths gaping, blowing hard after their mad, unscheduled flight. Dad ran across, taking great bounding strides to land on the plank beside Margaret.

Jack had been the culprit. During a refilling stop he'd somehow managed to get his hind leg over a chain and instead of behaving reasonably, which he rarely did anyway, had panicked and plunged about, causing the whole team to bolt. Margaret, even if she'd wanted to, couldn't have jumped clear because of the raking steel harrows coming behind and was in real danger of losing her footing and slipping forward off the plank onto the merciless discs: the possibilities didn't bear thinking about. So, instead of jumping or slipping, she did the thing her presence of mind dictated and hauled with all her might on the inside rein to pull that horse around and start them uphill where the going was too steep to continue at such a speed. And it worked. But later she told us that the worst part had been when Dad had joined her afterwards. He'd snatched the reins away violently in his agitation, jerking his arm back so violently that he'd unwittingly elbowed her in the stomach, completely winding her and rendering her breathless and speechless as well! She never did tell him what he'd done and he thought she was badly affected by the shock of what had happened and left it at that.

* * *

The other running away that nearly did for all of us was when the school bus almost came to grief. It was a sweltering Friday afternoon and the old vehicle was packed. Two elderly ladies took up the passenger seat alongside the driver, Mr. Carr, and jammed into a tiny seat at his right elbow was another passenger, a one-legged man who sat with his crutch stuck upright beside him. Mother, who'd been in town for a day's shopping, shared one of the narrow seats in the back of the bus with us children. Once we were all on board, the engine roared and spluttered, grey canvas blinds flapped, the bus slowly gathered speed and we were off at last, restive and eager at the idea of the weekend ahead. At first there was the usual scuffling and thumping down the back where the bigger boys and girls sat, but once out of town, they began to sing, the rest of us joining in where we could. Gradually the bus emptied as children were dropped off, the singing continued and our stop was next. We were bowling along a wide road approaching the base of a hill, getting near home, when Mr. Carr made a move to overtake a slow-moving army truck ahead. We were drawing alongside when, CRUNCH! - we were knocked sideways by the truck as it slewed carelessly out, the driver apparently unaware of our presence.

The bus lurched violently to the right. Loose gravel scattered, brakes screeched and through a sickly yellow haze I saw the startled faces of the other children as they clung to their narrow seats. A muffled roar filled the air and dust poured in through every window as we lurched over the embankment. We were headed directly for a steep banked section of the creek where it cut through the bottom of our Triangle Paddock. Children, mute and big-eyed with fright, hung on as the clumsy old bus blundered and crashed across gutters and bumps in its hectic and unscheduled flight, that seemed to us to go on forever.

Gradually as the ground levelled out, we started slowing down. Then, as if by a miracle, there was a last violent jolt as Mr. Carr's desperate efforts to pull us up succeeded. We'd come to a standstill not more than a few yards from the edge of the creek, hard by a scraggly wattle bush that had never before in its life had so much attention! We sat quietly at first, still and stiff but as movement and talking began, some of the little ones started to cry as the first numbing shock wore thin. One of the elderly lady passengers had fainted and the other had a thin stream of blood from a cut eyebrow, but miraculously, no-one was seriously hurt. Suddenly Dad's voice, loud and accusing, broke in on the scene. He'd been working on the harvester in a nearby paddock and had seen the bus leave the road. His wife and five children were on board and his long legs, driven by fear and despair, had him there almost as we pulled up. The team was abandoned to its own devices.

The young soldiers from the truck came down from the road, shaken and plainly scared and it was to the trembling driver that Dad addressed himself. It took some time for the bystanders to persuade him there was no point in carrying out his initial threat to knock the boy's head off, thus adding to the fracas. Once reassured that there'd be no physical repercussions, Mr. Carr, grey-faced with shock, went around the back of the bus to inspect the fuming gas-producer. In all the long years he was to ferry us in and out to school without accident or incident, this day must have taken on nightmare proportions for him. United from our moment of peril, we kids all piled out and crowded over to see how close we'd come to disaster and to exclaim over what could have happened but didn't. There was some wild conjecture about the part the one-legged man played in our safe delivery: some said that if he hadn't been there, we wouldn't have had a chance, as he'd helped by getting both hands to the handbrake while Mr. Carr managed the steering. Goodness knows what really happened, but we were safe and there was a good deal of good fortune in it for us, as it had been so close and the alternative would have been unthinkable.

We relived it all again over tea that night. It was a bit of excitement then, something to tell the kids at school about, though by Monday the novelty had worn off and no-one else was really interested anyway! As we went to bed that night, Dad said with great feeling, "You'd better all say your prayers before you go to sleep and thank God you're safe." And he meant it.

CHAPTER 12

Margaret and Bob were well into their teens by the time it was decided we four older ones should be tutored in some of the social graces, mainly in the form of ballroom dancing and playing tennis. Our neighbour, Joy Webber, was to be our mentor in both these arts and so it was arranged that we should ride over to Webber's on Saturday afternoons to be taken in hand and shown firstly "what to do with our feet" on the dance floor. Poor Joy, we really were raw material and she must have needed all her patience to cope with our tripping, giggling efforts before we mastered even the rudiments of dancing. But she persevered and many a Saturday afternoon from then on was spent scraping around in waltz time on Webber's front verandah as the sun sloped away towards its night's rest behind the sea and the windup gramaphone played "*The Blue Danube*", "*The Gold and Silver Waltz*" and "*Two Little Girls in Blue*".

But it wasn't all waltzing; there were the intricacies of the Maxina, the Gypsy Tap and the Pride of Erin to master and my poor head whirled with the effort of trying to keep up and my tripping was neither light nor fantastic. One afternoon, Jenny and I, concentrating grimly on some new manoeuvre, intent on watching our feet and not looking where we were going, went over the edge of the verandah, lurched down the front steps and landed on our backs in the geranium bed below! By the end of our tuition, however, Bob and Margaret were proficient enough to go to the occasional Saturday night dance in the Bluff Point Hall and later to the Druids' Hall in town, so they were on their way.

It was on Sundays that we used to go to Webber's to play tennis on a hard, red-earth court that was punctured by antholes and shaded by several rustling, leafy gum trees. This activity made a good deal more sense to me than stumbling over someone else's feet and falling into geranium beds, and we all caught on to the idea pretty quickly. Dad decided it was time now that we had our own colas court put down - or rather that we put it down ourselves as it was entirely a family effort, levelling, rolling and marking until at last it was ready for use. This court was to be a success beyond our wildest dreams and eventually became the focal point of our social life. We played on it every spare minute of the day and often when we should have been about other business; on days when it was so hot that the tarry surface bubbled under our feet and in the cool of the evening for just as long as we could see the ball by the sinking sun. Later there were heroes and heroines like Frank Sedgeman and Gorgeous Gussie Moran to inspire us to keep our efforts up. School friends and kids who lived nearby came to play on weekends and holidays and if ever a "luxury" justified its existence, that tennis court did.

Both the older ones had left school by now but stayed on at home to remain Dad's offsiders; in fact, with all the stock to handle, he couldn't have managed without them and certainly wasn't very keen to try. When eventually Margaret set her heart on going nursing, he persuaded her to stay on at home, saying she wouldn't like it much anyway, as he put it, "helping scaly old men on and off pots"! With her long plaits cut off and her wavy auburn hair clustered around her face, Mother said she "just missed out on being beautiful", but there wasn't much time for looking in mirrors and less to grieve over what so nearly might have been. By sheer energy and personality she managed to build up a degree of social life between the myriad jobs to be done at home. There was an active Repertory Club in town and though there was the problem of getting in and out regularly for rehearsals, this was to provide some outlet for her drive. Anyway, problems existed only to be overcome, so a couple of times a week, she'd ride over to the boundary with Webber's, hitch her horse to the fence, and have a ride to town with Joy.

The three-mile ride home after rehearsal was often late and very cold and on nights when cloud scudded across the face of the moon and wind stirred the branches of the gnarled wattle trees around the base of the hills, there was no time wasted. As they crouched, black and inscrutable, against the shadowy landscapes, the age-old hills took on a decidedly threatening aspect and the mare shied at everything that moved or stood still until she neared home. Sometimes we'd hear Margaret as she crept in the open door of the sleepout, boots in hand, to tumble gratefully into bed for all too few hours before it was time to start a new day, but more often than not, we slept through her nocturnal comings and goings and woke to find her safely in her bed every morning.

* * *

I believe it was nineteen forty-four that Dad brought home the first motor vehicle I remember, a tiny green utility that he had almost to fold himself in half to get into. Apart from a bone-shaking, iron-tyred tractor he'd borrowed briefly and chugged around the Cow Paddock on at about two miles an hour with kids and dogs rushing about in ecstasies of excitement, we'd never seen Dad drive anything but horses before and at first it seemed incredibly funny. Fancy Dad being able to drive! Fancy us having a car of our own! It was unbelievable, even if it wasn't new.

Actually, Dad had had a truck in the early days of his marriage and later Mother was to shudder with remembered horror as she recalled some of their trips to town in it. It had solid rubber tyres, was completely doorless, and open to the elements and was apparently halted more by simple loss of momentum than by anything to do with brake power! Imagine their hectic progress as they rumbled and plunged from one bump to the next on the then unmade road, companionable conversation being impossible over the engine noise and general rattles and thumps. I can almost hear Mother saying, "Oh Stuart, do be more careful!" And no wonder - for at least some of the time she would have had a babe in arms and later another on the way, plus a hat to hold in place, quite apart from any instinctive gripping of the seat for her own safety. It must have been a vast relief when eventually the whole thing literally fell into such disrepair that it couldn't be got going again and there was no question of affording spare parts if in fact they were available.

But the little green ute was to open quite a number of doors for us, mainly in the way of outings to the pictures - not frequently but at least now we weren't completely cut off from anything we really wanted to see or do and Mother, even though she never learned to drive herself, didn't have to rely on the school bus to get her to town on Fridays for shopping and visiting the Library. Before the school bus era, Mrs. Green or Mrs. Morrell had sometimes called in as they both drove, doing occasional messages for Mother if they were going to town or sometimes taking her in. Mrs. Morrell drove what I thought was a very dashing model with "wire wheels", as we called them, and a dicky seat at the back.

But those days were gone now and we were independent. Oh, those marvellous, exciting Saturday nights when we did forsake Hillbilly Roundup to crouch in the back of the ute, going to town for the pictures. We were so warmed with anticipation and the joyous feeling of freedom that even on cold nights we were impervious to the chill that wrapped around us. Along the way, lights gleamed from the houses scattered along the Bluff Point Road and we'd feel acutely sorry for those people because they weren't going to the pictures like us. On his first such outing, David was most concerned that Mother wasn't taking a candle or lantern. In his experience, no-one ever moved about at night unless thus equipped and he was quite sure we'd never see these mysterious pictures in the dark!

Greer Garson was my first goddess of the silver screen. She seemed so incredibly refined and dainty for want of a better word and I used to peer into the mirror on the sleepout wall at my freckled visage, willing there to be some resemblance, no matter how slight, to this marvellous creature; but there was none. All that looked back at me was me, and never a trace of Greer Garson - even with my fairly fruitful imagination. Anyway, she was soon deposed in my affections by Ingrid Bergman and others like Rita Hayworth, Gene Tierney, Merle Oberon, and Hedy Lamarr, whose name still to me signifies the essence of absolute glamour. After seeing her in "White Cargo", I hopefully swathed myself in an ancient bedspread, posturing dramatically, and dangled the gold bands from the tops of pickle jars in my ears to achieve the look of Tondalayo. But it didn't work. If anything, I looked less like Hedy Lamarr than I had like Greer Garson!

What queens they were, though, so far removed from us and so beautiful! We read about them in Photoplay Magazine and swapped their pictures with the kids at school who were all movie-mad too. Perhaps my judgement is clouded by nostalgia now but to me it seems they were good movies then too. Violence had no part in most of them and there was pure entertainment like "Home in Indiana" and "State Fair" with pretty Jeanne Craine: Donald O'Connor with his dancing feet and face that was always good for a laugh and Esther Williams who swam like a dream. And who could forget Sonja Henie, the pert-faced little skater who by her skill gave us perhaps more pleasure than any of them. It was grand fun, transporting us temporarily from our mundane round and taking us to a world so far removed that we went home silently wrapped in our own little cocoons of thought, reliving every magic moment as we bumped and drowsed in the back of the ute. Later, after we'd read the books, there was "*My Friend Flicka*", "*Lassie Come Home*", "*The Overlanders*" and "*Gone With the Wind*", to mention but a few favourites.

We acquired our first refrigerator about this time too, a kerosene-operated one as we still had no electricity. Bob brought it home one Friday afternoon in the back of the ute, tall and regal and gleamingly brand new. This was real luxury, there was no other word for it! A car, yes, most people had cars now, but fancy being able to have cold drinks and even ice-cream. About the only time we'd ever had it was when Dad had afforded us a treat at Hancock's Store at the West End Beach when we'd been staying at the beach cottage. As I remember, there were little flat-bottomed cups with fluted sides and you either had a penny or threepenny scoopful, depending on your finance. Anyway, once off-loaded from the ute, there was some consternation when it seemed that the wonderful new acquisition may not fit through the kitchen door. It was heavy and bulky with insulation and there was a good deal of heaving and puffing and manoeuvring before we had our way with it.

At last it was in, down at the far end of the kitchen, away from the stove and we stood back to admire it again and see the general effect. Lord, how shabby it made everything else look! Glistening benignly from amongst its setting of corrugated iron walls and pot-holed cement floor, it seemed quite out of place, as though some gigantic force had carried it a long way and put it down in the first available space before coming back to pick it up later! But we soon became used to it and anyway there wasn't much point in doing anything very radical to the old kitchen as the house obviously wasn't going to last forever. Jenny took over the responsibility of fuelling and defrosting the fridge and made deep trays of delicious ice-cream for Sundays. It was almost too good to be true.

* * *

And there were more miracles of modern science - or plumbing at least yet to come. The water supply from the Ram Paddock soak had proved unsatisfactory, so a bore with a windmill was put down in the Long Paddock and at last a permanent, reliable water supply was available for the house. With finance becoming more readily available and enough water, there was now no impediment to having a proper toilet attached to the house and, when this became a reality, I think it was the greatest "convenience" of all, for everyone. Imagine, no more perilous night trips climbing through the wire fence in flapping dressing gowns while shielding a guttering candle in one hand -- just a discreet disappearance out through the back door of the kitchen, around the corner and off the end of the bathroom. It was enough to make one go sometimes simply for the wonder of being able to pull that magical chain!

In time, the pit by the creek was filled in and the old building was pushed over - seeming to totter briefly in mild protest before giving in to the inevitable and crashing ignominiously to the ground. It was pulled away then behind the wagon, spiders and all, to be broken up for salvage of any of its still useful parts.

* * *

It was getting on to the end of the war when Doug came into the picture. He was one of a number of Italian prisoners of war sent out to work on farms in the district: a dapper little man with a neat toothbrush moustache and a flash of gold that twinkled in a front tooth. Doug was short for Douguana, or at least that was how it sounded to us and he nodded his acceptance of the diminutive with a grave smile. He'd been captured in North Africa and it was hard to imagine this

David and Doug, our friendly Italian prisoner of war.

neat, courteous little man as being a former enemy. Only the faded red, ill-fitting prisoner's garb which he wore at all times, betrayed him. Cassino, in the south of Italy, was his hometown and whatever his pre-war occupation had been, farming Australian style was way outside his range of experience. But in his quiet way he at least learned to earn his keep and make himself useful.

Doug had all his meals with us and, sometimes after tea in the evening, sat with the family in the dining room to listen to the radio before retiring to his room not far from the house. We soon came to regard the presence of this mild little man as a part of our daily life and whenever we went to church or the pictures, Doug came too, crouching with the rest of us in the back of the ute. He seemed particularly fond of David, whom he called "Daywood" and who, with his dark eyes and olive skin, could certainly have been taken for a child of the Mediterranean, and Doug had no sons of his own. After he'd been with us for a while, he indicated one evening that there was something he'd like to show us, and we gathered around the kitchen table not knowing quite what to expect. First, from several layers of tissue paper, he produced a number of pencil sketches of his wife, a solemn, dark-eyed woman, then another of her surrounded by five little girls in white dresses. They were copied from a family group photograph and sketched onto thick, white paper with infinite care and considerable talent. We were really very impressed and Doug's front tooth flashed and winked in appreciation as we admired not only his handiwork, but his fine family.

Then the rustling tissue paper yielded the prize exhibits. On stiff pieces of canvas which he explained he'd cut off his tent while a P.O.W. in Africa, he'd embroidered pictures of the Madonna and Child and various saints. By employing all his native ingenuity, he'd managed to collect enough threads to give a variety of colours, and though the drawings were crude, the needlework was quite exquisite. Only one thing detracted from the reverence of the occasion. One of the saintly ladies was depicted proffering her eyes on a platter: but not only her eyes. Above them were a pair of delicately arched and clearly astonished eyebrows! Jenny and I clung to each other, almost choking with suppressed laughter and not daring to catch Mother's eye. Gigglers that we were, it was never far below the surface and this was just too much. Mother somehow managed to keep the attention away from us and I hope Doug never noticed.

When the news of Mussolini's death came through, Dad broke it to Doug, unsure of the effect it might have on him. He needn't have worried, one way or the other. Doug smiled patiently and said quite positively, "No. Ees not true." Dad persisted, feeling he'd been misunderstood, but the little man was adamant. It wasn't true. Dad told Mother incredulously, "The little blighter didn't believe me!" So the disbeliever was invited to hear for himself on the news after tea. But he was unmoved and spread his hands in a gesture of disdain, haltingly declaring, "Ees all prop-a-ganda. Ees not true!" For him his leader still lived and all was as before in Cassino, which in fact by this time had been utterly ravaged by war.

Then the day he longed for came at last, the first step on the long road to home and we wished him well, as we saw him go on the truck that came around collecting prisoners from the farms in our district. There was plenty to keep our minds busy as well as our hands after he'd gone but sometimes Mother would wonder aloud how Doug had found things back in his beloved beleaguered Cassino; how things were with his calm-eyed wife and five little girls in white and she shuddered to think of the devastation that had taken place since he'd last seen his home. Often Mother would get up and leave the room when the news from either side was too distressing. She abhorred violence in any fashion and the memories of those lost in the Great War, the senseless, crushing futility of it all and the wounds that never healed, overcame her.

Soon the war was over. I was twelve then, in sixth standard at school and strangely, have no particular memory of being told. Half my short life had been lived to the accompaniment of it; punctuated several times daily by the News. Terms like Fuzzy Wuzzy Angel, Doodlebug, and Blackout were quite familiar, so too were place names like Dunkirk, Potsdam, Port Moresby, Tobruk and, mainly through Doug, Cassino. With the new peace came a time to weep again for those who weren't coming back and for those who had suffered so terribly. But the historians have dealt with that so much more adequately than I could ever hope to.

Back on the home front, quite a long time later, a strange letter arrived.

Grubby with fingerprints and much handled in transit, it was from Doug, a plea to help him come back to Australia, with or without his family I don't remember now. There was nothing much that could be done: Europe was in post-war chaos. So the letter was sent with an explanation to the appropriate authorities but we heard nothing further. I wonder if he ever made it.

* * *

Bob was the first of the family to fly the nest. He was eighteen just after the war finished and grieved because he'd not been old enough to join up. He headed now for Kalgoorlie and his first taste of life outside farming. Granny moved back to town to share a house with one of her widowed friends and for the first time, Margaret had a room to herself. With Grandpa long gone, we felt we were quite a small family with only six of us around the kitchen table.

CHAPTER 13

Suddenly it was nineteen forty-six and time to uproot myself from the comfortable and familiar environs of Primary School and the teacher Miss Eastlake who had guided us through sixth standard with such interest and enthusiasm, and embark on a High School career which was to be, to say the least, undistinguished. English had never been a problem for me, history became all the more interesting for the dynamic approach of Miss Richards, but secondary school mathematics got quite out of hand! Algebra evoked in me an insurmountable mental block and my only concern during geometry lessons was to avoid Mr. Andrew's glance as he scanned the assembled class before selecting one of us to go out to the front of the room and work out a geometric theorem for him on the blackboard. So great was the turmoil within me before he made his selection and even greater the flood of relief that overwhelmed me when, every time he chose other than me, that there was literally no time left to concentrate on the subject itself. Consequently, I failed dismally and continually in geometry.

Trigonometry was a mess. Anyway, I could never imagine when in the foreseeable future I would need to know how to measure a flagpole on a building or a tower on a hill, so gave it even less attention than geometry. Dear, gentle Miss Shearing taught us typing, shorthand and art and, through her own quiet enthusiasm for the latter, managed to promote a degree of keenness in me, though in still art I managed nothing better than a series of lopsided jugs and curiously bulbous bottles. My bowls of flowers looked literally like "dry arrangements", but weren't meant to.

Recess and lunchtimes at High School were largely filled in with some kind of sporting or physical activity. There was no canteen at the school and there would have been precious little money to spend at it if there had been, so apart from the library, which was not particularly well-stocked by today's standards, there were few other diversions. Knuckle-jacks, hoppy, skippy and film stars had all been left behind at Primary School. So generally we went down to the oval at the back and play softball or practised for Sport's Day or, if the boys would let us, joined in a game of cricket or football. But there was just one day in every year when the lunchtime routine was quite different and that was on Melbourne Cup Day.

Then, immediately the lunch bell rang, anyone interested would disappear from the school grounds. Our trek took us on a path worn down sandhills, past scraggly boxthorn bushes, across a flat covered in squashy "pig face", past St. Xavier's Cathedral, the Bishop's Palace, Young Motors, around the corner past the Wise Owl Tearooms, cutting across in front of the Elite Supply Drapery to Lupp's Music Shop. Here a statuesque and exotic lady with dark, drawn-back hair and slumbrous eyes stood near the doorway fondling a snuffling Pekinese that lay perpetually cradled in her braceleted arms. Musical instruments glinted tantalisingly in the shop behind her; a set of drums, a trumpet, guitars and harmonicas and a piano that stood open with the ivories gleaming and sheet music lying open and about on shelves. Something "different" there was about that shop - not a place to be entered into lightly, not that we would have had any business there anyway. But on Melbourne Cup Day, diffidence was cast aside and mystery didn't seem to be so daunting. There'd be a cluster of us on the pavement just outside Lupp's doorway where the radio was tuned in and turned up to cover the big race and it was here that we heard the champions of the day bring home the bacon. It just seemed so important to know; not that any of us ever laid a bet or would have known how to and there was no money to change hands. As soon as it was over, we all made the journey back to school quite happily, arriving just in time to beat the bell.

* * *

The last of the domestic marvels that became a reality for our household around the end of the war was the electricity generated by a small engine which puttered and banged away in a shed near the house. Oh, the wonder of being able to press a switch or pull a cord for instant light.

But how frustrating those cords could be when standing in the middle of the vast empty blackness of the sleepout, groping. Your hand would only have to knock the bakelite knob at the end of the cord once to send it spinning off into ever-widening circles, gathering momentum with any random contact. The only thing to do then was to wait as patiently as possible for the action to die down and then start again, stalking that elusive giver of light like a mime artist on a darkened stage!

But it was easier and I suppose quicker than lighting lamps, beautiful as they were in their own way, casting such a soft glow that even our old dining room was flattered into some degree of nocturnal beauty. I remember feeling sad when the big main lamp with the coaching scene around the shade was lit for the last time. Mother packed the lamps away in a big box after that, lingering over the task, no doubt thinking back on the countless times she'd filled and cleaned them, trimming the wicks, changing the mantles and washing the tall glasses with infinite care. The words were different but the sentiments were the same as in the old hillbilly song, "The Lonesome Trail Ain't Lonesome Anymore". We were moving along with the times, perhaps a step or two behind most others, but moving just the same; daily living tasks were being made easier and some small, time-consuming rituals were being put behind us, never to be repeated. It was progress sure enough, but somehow things would never be the same again.

One thing, however, that no-one could grieve over not being the same was the ironing. Up till now, Mother had only ever had a selection of flat irons and a couple of Mrs. Pott's, all of which had to be heated on top of the stove. She must have tracked backwards and forwards for hundreds of miles over the years, between the table and the stove, lifting and replacing those irons. To keep the surfaces smooth, she used the butt-end of a candle, melted onto a pad of clean rag and when as a little girl I used to pull up a chair and hang over the end of the table to watch her iron, I loved the clean, hot smell of melting candle-grease as she briskly rubbed the iron on it before starting again. Drip-dry garments were a long way off then and most cottons had to be starched and ironed with care. It was a business, but one afternoon or morning a week was set aside for the purpose, and for a small child at least, it was a companionable atmosphere and nothing short of fascinating to see the dampened, crumpled fabric emerging crisp and smooth with every movement of the iron. From the user's point of view, though, there could have been little room for sentiment, and the electric iron was a real step forward.

* * *

There was a great boom on the tomato market around the end of the war and Dad decided we should capitalise on it while it lasted. We had all the land we needed and plenty of labour, so a few acres were fenced and brought under cultivation down by the dam, with good soil and drainage and adequate water for most of the season. Cropping was abandoned, the team horses were turned out to "eat their heads off" and the chaff house was set up as a packing shed with bins for grading and benches for packing and making cases. In due course, many an evening was spent, "packing for Melbourne". Uncle Hubert, Mother's brother, moved out from town to work the garden with Dad on a share basis, staying in the little room that Doug had lived in before him.

Sometimes after school and certainly on weekends there was enough planting out, pruning, watering and picking to keep us all busy and instead of cutting chaff on Sundays, our fingers stank of tomato sap and bluestone and I for one grumbled mightily and longed for the days when Dad took the team out seeding on Pipeclay Hill. It was even a treat to have to cart water when the dam was pumped out as it was at least a jaunt away from the garden and a chance to straighten up; to day-dream a while as old Kate and Blossom dawdled along, heads down and tails swishing and no-one wanting to hurry them too much. For all our grumbling, however, the garden was a great success financially and Dad said we made more money out of those few acres than he'd ever made out of all his years of farming. Bob was back now too after a couple of years away, a handsome, much-matured and mellowed young man with a diesel certificate from the School of Mines in Kalgoorlie. He was given to crooning love songs as he worked tirelessly amongst the tomatoes or on the little Farmall tractor that had replaced big Caesar and the single furrow plough for convenience and manoeuvrability in the garden.

It was during the "garden era" that Dad decided on a degree of personal emancipation in the form of wearing shorts for the first time in his life. Previously, his long legs had always been encased in either moleskins, army trousers or dungarees and suddenly, he was tired of it. So one day he appeared before our astonished gaze with as much nonchalance as he could muster, in the remains of a pair of old trousers that looked as if they'd been hacked off above the knees with a pair of dagging shears! This was the way he declared, to our giggles and outright laughter, everyone should wear shorts. No more long trousers for him! Even Mother, who seemed to us to be a most unlikely recruit, was not exempt from his persuasion and he strode off to the garden that day revelling in his new-found freedom, unmindful of her dire warnings about sunburn.

It beat down steadily that day, deliciously warm at first, then stinging a little on thighs that hadn't felt the sun since boyhood all those years before. It wasn't until evening that the full effect was felt and obvious and then warnings were too late. But to cut a long story short, having weathered that first bad case, Dad decided it would be wise to take the sun in small doses after that and looked about for some method of "breaking things up a bit". His eyes lit on a faded pink kimono-type cotton gown that had been Granny's and was light and cool and easily tucked into the waist band of his "shorts", giving a wafting, skirt-like effect. The sight that met our eyes then had to be seen to be believed. The entire family fell about laughing, clinging to each other as we doubled up till our faces ached and our eyes streamed. In the face of such unrestrained hilarity, it was Dad's turn to act with impatience and disdain and there were dark mutterings of "Damn fools. Standing around ... Laughing at a man ...!" As he strode off towards the garden like an angry emu, the kimono bunched at the back, twitching with every stride into what looked absurdly like an indignant pink bustle!

'But if we have been overcome by laughter, it was hard to judge what the gardeners felt about being confronted by this spectacle, as their only reaction was stunned silence. Several times we noticed them down at their pumps, looking this way and that through the trees as Dad defiantly tore about on the Farmall or strode, flapping and fluttering pinkly up and down to the dam to stop or start our pump. Not a single snigger seemed to emanate from behind that thin screen of trees, and I think that, far from being amused, they were more concerned that their hitherto quite reasonable neighbour had suddenly taken leave of his senses, therefore anything might happen!

In time, of course, wind, sun and dogged perseverance won out and at last Dad's legs were tanned to a most admirable degree. Then the old kimono was put aside and Mother eventually persuaded him to buy himself a couple of pairs of decent shorts; otherwise I'm sure he would have gone along quite happily "making do" with his frightful homemade jobs from then on. Really, for a good-looking person, he was most amazingly unconscious and uncaring about clothes and even when he would have been able to spend more money on himself and his appearance, this was always done most grudgingly; he preferring to cling to familiar things and wear them patched and repatched till they literally fell to pieces about him. Not that he was mean, but I guess it was hard after all those years of scraping along, to change. After all, he reminded us many times that we'd been raised and the farm had been run on £3-00 a week from the Bank and what we could produce and do ourselves and I should image that after that, fussing about new clothes seemed to him a kind of monstrous vanity.

Meanwhile, the little green ute which had charmed us so and given us so much pleasure as a runabout, had proved quite inadequate for general farm work. The wagon still had to be used for carting wood, water or anything in bulk. So it was decided to replace it with something more practical and sizeable. This "something" turned out to be a great snub-nosed, tawny-green ex-army truck that looked huge after the diminutive utility and as far as I can remember, lived up to all that was expected of it. After this there were beach picnics sometimes at the weekend when we'd join forces with friends to swim and play cricket on the hard, unspoiled whiteness of the West End beach.

Thinking of the truck also brings to mind Joe, who came to work for Dad about that time. He was a Cockney lad who'd jumped ship in Fremantle and was looking for work to tide him over. As it turned out, Joe wasn't too keen on work, whatever the need, but he was a good-natured enough lad and regaled us with accounts of the street fights his mother embroiled herself and her family in back in Bermondsey with great relish and probably a whole lot of embroidery. She was "loovly", his Moom, he said, "She 'ad red 'air and book teeth" and could apparently, throw a flat iron further than anyone else's Moom in the street! He seemed to me such a man of the world and talked frequently of his adventures, real or imagined, in "Yankeeland", but at heart perhaps he was just a kid adrift in the world, a long way from home and homesick for his Mum and familiar things.

We'd always been admonished not to ride on the back of the truck with our legs dangling over the side as this was dangerous going through gates or along fences, also to keep clear of the tail end of the tray in case we bounced right off whilst going along. Joe, however, always one to play to an audience, flouted these restrictions and, while in progress, would entertain us with a soft shoe shuffle, standing as far back to the rear as possible with his hands in his pockets, rolling his googly eyes as he sang, "Chattanooga Choo Choo", all the go in Yankeeland, he assured us. Dad would roar at him to sit down if he saw him, but as Bob mostly drove the truck now, he went merrily on, heeding no warnings and being lucky.

I wonder what became of Joe and of others who came to mind in passing; of a red-haired, freckle-faced lad of about twelve who turned up one wet and stormy night, barefoot, cheerful and soaked to the skin, "runnin' away from the old man", on a skinny old horse that looked as if it didn't have much of a mind for runnin' anywhere, let alone on such a night. Both were taken in, dried out and fed and neither looked to be in any hurry to move on. After several days, the father turned up, riding a black mare and with a stockwhip coiled menacingly over one shoulder. The prodigal son dutifully thanked Mother and Dad for everything and caught and mounted his aged steed. Few words were exchanged on either side and after a tacit nod from the parent, they moved off, the kid apparently quite cheerfully going back to "the old man" and all he'd been at such pains to get away from only a few nights before.

There was someone else who flitted briefly on the outskirts of my being - a one-legged man who rode a fine bay horse and carried a crutch hooked over the kneepad of his saddle as he rode. For a while we saw him almost daily as we chugged and flapped along the Glenfield Road in the school bus and he'd wave to us as he went; cantering, cantering on his bright bay gelding. He was quite young and no doubt a casualty of the war, tough and cheerful and a fine horseman.

Then, as suddenly as he'd come, he went. I used to look out for him, just to wave and be waved at as a simple daily ritual of communication and to admire his skill in handling his horse, but he'd gone and the trips to school and back were the duller for his going.

* * *

At last the garden era was over. Uncle Hubert moved back to town and the tomato sticks were pulled out and laid in great heaps on the ground. The brush fencing was to stand resolutely on, shielding its phantom charges for several more years, livestock wandering in and out of where the neat rows of tomatoes had once flourished. The garden had served its purpose admirably, but I for one had no sentiment to spare for it or anything to do with it. Perhaps this was some kind of snobbery; we were farmers, not gardeners and farming was what we should have been about instead of being side-tracked. And if the garden era was over for us, so too was the era of the draught horse drawing to a close. I believe that after this, the team was brought in and used for only one more season before being replaced by a kerosene burning Massey Harris tractor which had a shed built specially to house it and Bob fussing over it like a hen with one chick, recording daily in a logbook its working hours, oil changes - every mood and heartbeat it seemed.

The horses were around for quite a long time to come, just feeding and getting fat. I'm sure Dad put off their disposal for as long as was possible. They'd been good, loyal friends and had worked long, hard hours in our service and it must have been hard for him to see them go. But go they had to, as otherwise the place would have been cluttered up with a lot of aged and decrepit horses staggering about on their last legs, and there was no room for maudlin sentiment.

Later I realised this reluctance on Dad's part could have stemmed from the fact that when they left France at the end of the war, the horses had to be destroyed. There was no alternative as they couldn't be brought back to Australia of turned loose in such great numbers to forage for themselves on the devastated countryside of France. Imagine the heartbreak at the awful slaughter of such faithful, trusting friends, including Kitty, the little black mare. No wonder he didn't talk much about it: he never was one for "going on" about things anyway.

I don't remember seeing any of them leave, it was always during school hours and nothing much was said, though I'm sure poor Margaret must have had some heart-rending errands as she rode away leading them from her hack. Then suddenly we'd realise that some were missing; Peggy and Captain, Biddy and Baldy, Kate and Blossom, Jack and Caesar and so on until only the saddle horses were left. I did find out much later that Dad had arranged for someone else to dispose of them, not selling them but retaining ownership so they couldn't be resold. They'd done their life's work and he didn't want someone else flogging them about to get the last out of them but for them to go out quickly and in good condition. So that was how it was in the end and down in the harness shed, rows of winker bridles and collars rested idly on their pegs and rails, never to be used again, hardening with age and gently gathering dust and cobwebs.

CHAPTER 14

Inevitably our family was growing up and out now. Bob was home but it was time for the older girls to take jobs in town. Jenny was the first, going straight from school to the office at Dalgety's. She boarded in town with Granny during the week and came home for weekends, blonde and pretty and neat as a pin. Margaret's first job was as receptionist at a Hair Salon. It was so good to have the family complete again on these weekends when the girls came home; somehow reassuring that things weren't changing too much or too fast. And there was always so much to do, news to exchange and be caught up with. The tennis court worked overtime, Saturday night by the radio still held the same appeal, at least for David and me, and on Sunday mornings the volume was turned up to take the weekly Hit Parade from 6GE, Geraldton. These were the days of Perry Como, Vaughan Munro, Dinah Shore, Jo Stafford and Guy Lombardo, to mention a few. After this there were salad lunches with delicious thick dressing made with condensed milk and trays of ice-cream to follow and the atmosphere seemed charged with good spirits and expectancy and, most of all, just being together because all too soon it would be time to disperse again for the coming week.

With the advent of everyone's mobility, Miss Biddle had long since ceased her monthly Sunday afternoon visits and instead they were taken up with callers from town, friends of Bob's and the girls who came out in their carloads to play tennis and sip tea under the shade of the big, leafy fig trees that ran down one side of the court. Often at afternoon tea time there weren't enough cups to go around and everything that even remotely resembled one was pressed into service. No-one seemed to mind the occasional necessity for drinking from an enamel pannikin that had seen better days or a chipped bunny mug and in the end, Mother bought an outsized teapot such as caterers use, to cope with the flow. Occasionally some of the visitors would stay for tea as well and these Sunday evenings were rounded off with bowls of thick, meaty soup from one of Mother's boilers. They were grand times; plenty of fun and lighthearted banter - an outing for the folks from town and a fresh, new change for we who were still at home.

* * *

A number of our Macedonian contemporaries were married by now and we had been invited to most of their weddings, which were solemnised in the Church of England in town. Afterwards the celebrations moved invariably to the packing shed of one of the families involved, where the men seemed to do ninety per cent of the celebrating and the largely black-clad women, seated together in the more dimly lit recesses of the shed, seemed to an observer's eye to have a very dull time of it. Even the little bride in her pristine white glory was fairly inconspicuous in the scheme of things once the ceremony was over: but that was how it seemed to us, and I guess in their own way she was queen for a day even if she would be out picking tomatoes with the rest tomorrow.

Certainly, it was the men who did all the dancing at these functions once things warmed up, moving in a circle, hands linked by handkerchiefs held between them, shuffling in time to the music that to me held a strange, wild lament. There was a novel method of paying the musicians who as far as I can

David and Jenny with tennis court in background.

remember were all locals. At intervals throughout the evening, the menfolk would stroll over, lick a ten shilling or one pound note and, with a fitting flourish, slap it on the forehead of the music-maker of his choice, who never batted an eyelid, but plucked or tootled or drummed doggedly on, whatever his instrument happened to be, without change of expression. As can be imagined, as the evening wore on and the atmosphere grew more convivial and exuberant, the flourish and the notes became more flamboyant and frequent, until sometimes a musician literally ran out of face and the enthusiastic donor would have to roll his note up tight and stick it behind or into an ear, all to the accompaniment of cheers and encouragement from the rest of the assembly. With such healthy competition and the feeling of good fellowship abroad, I imagine some of the musicians went home considerably better off for such an evening and possibly some revellers from the night before woke up the next day to wonder just what had happened to their paper money.

* * *

At that time, Friday afternoon was the highlight of many a country family's week as this was when all and sundry came to town to shop, have lunch perhaps if they came from a good way out, and generally see everyone else who was in town for the same purpose. Now, any day does for shopping, as it's easy enough to run in and out, but then, Friday was special and if for any reason you couldn't make it, there was a definite feeling of having missed out. The main street was full of people and traffic as farmers and gardeners exchanged comments on crops and weather and everything that concerns men of the soil, and women caught up on neighbours and friends they rarely saw at other times. There was good fellowship and optimism in the air with the war well over, and even if you didn't actually know everyone you saw, at least you greeted one another and there was such a strong feeling of belonging that no-one could ever have imagined then, going back and feeling like a stranger in your own town later in life. But then no-one could have foreseen the growth of the town either.

We children came down to join our parents after school and the treat of the day for us would be a "spider" at one of the Greek Cafes; a generous scoop of ice-cream that fizzed and bobbed when added to a tall, thick milkshake glass full of cool drink. During the afternoon, Mother would have a cup of tea at the Wise Owl Tearooms and one of her main ports of call would be to the Mechanic's Institute Library with the huge Moreton Bay fig trees outside and the horse water trough near the footpath in front. With everything done, it was off home in time to do the milking, collect eggs and perhaps feed lambs before sundown so there was no "standing about", as Dad called it.

* * *

At last it was time for me to leave school, and I did so without regret, though completely in the dark about what course my life should take in the immediate or even far distant future. There seemed to be no urgency for me to come to any rapid decisions, so I thankfully retired to the comfortable and familiar surroundings of home to give a hand where necessary and take every day as it came. One of the big interests in my life at this time was cricket, something Dad had fostered over the years from when I had first shown an interest and when the Australians were playing Test Matches overseas, I sat up with him to listen and follow their fortunes with bated breath. Scrap books bulged with pictures and articles cut out of papers and magazines and "*Sporting Life*" replaced "*Photoplay*" in my priorities from then on. They were great days with heroes like Lindwall, Miller, Bradman, Toshack and Tallon to recall but a few and I am ever grateful for this facet of life that has and will always add such interest for me and so many others.

* * *

Well, that's about it really; not much of a story, more like a sentimental journey for me. Memories and impressions of a childhood I wouldn't have exchanged for a king's ransom and something in the way of a tribute to my parents and many others like them who worked hard to raise their families; and the kids who worked too, often labouring at tasks way beyond what should have been expected of them and giving up any chance of furthering personal ambition to help Dad on the farm or in the shop or wherever needed, whether they liked it or not. Not much chance then to "do your own thing"; it was more a matter of simple survival and who is to say things were any the worse for that? And perhaps it's a tribute too to an era when, of necessity, the pace of life was slower and even if it wasn't better for everyone in every way, at least we had time to sit in the sun awhile, to talk to each other and enjoy the few things we did have.

One thing I've realised as I've gone along is that I could recall people, events and general impressions from way back when I was a small child far more easily than I could from, say, fourteen on. After that there are quite a few gaps and blanks and things become more generalised and harder to keep in sequence. But there was one evening that will stay with me forever; it was just before I left home to work in the city and I'd been for my last ride. Afterwards, I unsaddled my horse at the harness shed and jumped on him to canter bareback up the fenceline to just under the hill where the young pilot had stumbled and slithered from his crashed aircraft years before. The horse was impatient to be free and bumped and rubbed his head wearily against me as I slipped the bridle off and patted his sweaty neck.

It was just on dusk; a calm, perfect evening late in September and sheep were coming around the base of the hill to drink at the trough, walking one behind the other, heads down, in the peculiarly single-minded, bustling way that sheep have when they're doing something they want to do. Little puffs of fine dust spurted up from their small, busy hooves and hung in a haze above them, silhouetted against the eastern sky. The sturdy little Merino, Dad called them; kick them, cut them and starve them, then test them with fire, flood and drought and like as not they'd survive, he'd say. Australia owed an inestimable debt to the sturdy little Merino. I watched them silently as I stood there with the still warm bridle over my shoulder and the inside of my trousers clinging damply to my legs. There was a smell of horse and earth and sheep and dust; all the familiar smells of childhood ---like the creek on a summer day - and in a surge of choking, overwhelming nostalgia, was the sure knowledge that things could never be the same; this moment could never come again.

A big, knobbly rock lay nearby and I perched on it, reluctant to hasten the inevitable. There was so much to think back on up there in the quiet shadow of the hill with only the incurious sheep to observe me. I looked down to where the ugly, ungracious old house crouched by the creek as smoke spiralled lazily from the chimney. Mother was in the kitchen and all was well with the world. We'd had so much fun and laughter in the old place. Probably we were easily amused for after all, we'd never been used to sophisticated entertainment, but there was always laughter. Very often it was the means of getting us into trouble with Dad, who was tired at the end of a long day and sometimes left the table in disgust when one or more of us girls got the giggles: like the time Jenny put out the lamp on the tea table with a mouthful of soup explosively ejected after valiantly trying to control herself!

Further up the creek where the "will-yarks" uttered their strange, wild cry, was the spot where the old dub had leaned and listened for so many years and where the spider orchids still flourished under the big gum tree that used to reach out and scratch the tin roof of the old building on those hazardous night visits when we were small. The Mail Gate road wound lumpily up the Long Paddock beside the darkening creek, and down past the house, towards the dam, nothing much had changed since Louis, straight-backed in his black hat and dark suit, had jolted home with his hard-boiled eggs, behind the drooping La La; and Mother's Little Man had creaked up in his cart with something special for Mother.

Many of the gardeners had gone now, moving to areas closer to town and we missed seeing them going up the road on their way to town on Friday morning with the young women and girls in their brightly-coloured dresses, chattering and laughing on the back of the trucks. The little homes were empty and the brush fences stood sturdily on with only weeds and the ever-blowing wind as their companions. We'd had good neighbours all round and on every side; we'd shared their hospitality and their minor calamities and helped each other out in times of need and stress. There can be no better neighbours than that.

I looked away across the valley towards the hill where Grandpa rode as a boy to watch and wait for his mother. The shadows were long there now and also in the Clover Paddock where the team had once bolted with Margaret and where the horses had often been turned out to graze when not being worked. There was a clump of Christmas trees in the Clover Paddock that flamed annually with their fiery, orange blossom, spectacular and sweet, but on closer inspection, swarming with ants attracted to that sweetness. The horses loved to chew and gnaw at the pithy wood of the Christmas trees and eventually completely ring-barked the whole lot so that Dad had to push them over one by one as they were in danger of toppling over onto the stock and perhaps hurting them. And nearer the house in the Cow Paddock, Jenny and David and I had made cubbies and nests and tunnels in the great stands of dandelion that grew there every spring. Often the days were warm and the sound of the bees as they went about their business, made one feel so overpoweringly drowsy that quite often our activities ended with us curling up small amongst the warm, crushed stems and going to sleep. And I thought as I sat there, that though this moment could never come again and no matter what was ahead, no-one could ever take away what had been or spoil the memory of it.

Sounds floated up to me now; a dog barked and a calf, locked away from its mother for the night, bawled mournfully. Dad was walking back from his evening inspection of the tank at the mill in the Long Paddock. I could just make out his long form in the last of the light, hat as always, firmly on his head and walking with his curiously loose-limbed gait, as someone once said, "as though he was all tacked together". It was too dark now to see the smoke rising from the chimney and a light gleamed from the kitchen side of the house. It was a weekend and everyone was home; tea would be ready and perhaps they'd be wondering where I was. I stood up at last. Childhood was over and it was time to go.